SEP 1 3 2012

W9-CKM-618

MONSTER

BY THE SAME AUTHOR

A Killer's Essence
The Caretaker of Lorne Field
Outsourced
Killer
Small Crimes
Pariah

MONSTER

A Novel of Frankenstein

DAVE ZELTSERMAN

The Overlook Press
New York, NY

This edition first published in hardcover in the United States in 2012 by

The Overlook Press, Peter Mayer Publishers, Inc.
141 Wooster Street
New York, NY 10012
www.overlookpress.com
For bulk and special sales, please contact sales@overlookny.com

Copyright © 2012 by Dave Zeltserman

All rights reserved. No part of this publication may be reproduced or transmitted in any form or by any means, electronic or mechanical, including photocopy, recording, or any information storage and retrieval system now known or to be invented, without permission in writing from the publisher, except by a reviewer who wishes to quote brief passages in connection with a review written for inclusion in a magazine, newspaper, or broadcast.

Cataloging-in-Publication Data is available from the Library of Congress

Book design and typeformatting by Bernard Schleifer
Manufactured in the United States of America
ISBN 978-159020-860-1

To the memory of my father,
Samuel Zeltserman

Monster

PROLOGUE

For far too many years Victor Frankenstein's outrageous fabrication has stood unchallenged. I cannot blame Captain Walton for his role in this, for he was most likely an honorable man who was duped by Frankenstein's egregious lies; lies told for no other reason than to save the reputation and name of a sinister and black-hearted man, a man who had willingly spent his life in the service of the devil. Nor can I blame Mary Shelley for further putting these lies to paper once they had found their way to her. The truth, though, is that Frankenstein was hardly the tragic figure that he so skillfully presented to Captain Walton, nor did he create his abomination out of a youthful but misguided obsession. Instead, he was a man of a most depraved nature and spirit; his true intention being to create his own Hell on earth. I know all of this because I, Friedrich Hoffmann of Ingolstadt, am the very same abomination that Frankenstein brought forth into the world. And, despite my hardest efforts, I have not been able to leave it.

Although the events that I put forth in this journal took place over two hundred years ago, they are still quite vivid in my mind. Victor Frankenstein's villainous acts were numerous, as were his unfortunate victims, among whose ranks I can chiefly be included. I hope that I can now put his lies to rest and that the world will finally understand the true story, as horrible as it is.

As I write this, I can only pray that Frankenstein's twisted soul is rotting in whatever crevice within Hell it has surely sunk into.

—FRIEDRICH HOFFMANN

CHAPTER 1

First my feet were broken.

Then my ankles.

After that it was my shins. The cudgel's next targets were my knees, shattering them as well.

I screamed, of course. I screamed with the first blow and I screamed with each additional one. How could any man being broken on the wheel not? Over my screams I heard the crowd that had been so exuberantly jeering for my blood silence themselves as if on command. For a moment it was only my screaming that filled the air. The moment did not last.

"Confess, Friedrich Hoffmann. Confess while you are still able to!"

The priest was once again demanding my confession. He had been the one to silence the crowd and momentarily stay the executioner's hand.

Using every ounce of strength I had I stopped my screaming so that I could answer him.

"Am I to confess to a crime of which I am innocent?" I asked him through my ragged breathing. "Especially a crime as wicked as the one of which I am being accused? Would that not be a greater sin?"

I forced myself to meet the priest's cold eyes. Eyes that held not a drop of pity.

"You will die without absolution if you do not confess," he warned me in his thunderous voice. "Your unredeemed soul to be condemned to Hell. Confess now!"

I looked away from him and did not answer. I could hear a grunt escape from the executioner's lips and then my thigh bones were shattered. With that blow the roar of the crowd swallowed me up.

Madness would have been a welcome release, but somehow it never came. Even after the executioner had broken my hips and moved on to my upper body, the madness stubbornly refused to rescue me.

Deep within my heart I prayed.

My beloved Johanna, you must believe that I am innocent of what they claim. Death does not worry me, only the fear that these false accusations will keep me from you.

The blows from the cudgel had stopped. The priest kneeled by me so that his awful face was near mine, his lips moving in a cruel manner. I was beyond hearing. Instead I was engulfed within a cacophony of sounds. The roar of the crowd, the priest's words, my own screaming, all blending together into a deafening roar. Soon the priest disappeared and the executioner took his place. Just as all noises had blended together, so too did all my pain blend together. I wasn't even aware that the executioner had sliced open my arms so that my mangled bones could be braided to the spokes of the wheel. It wasn't until the wheel was lifted and I was suspended by my broken arms that I understood that this had happened, but the pain no longer mattered. I was beyond that. I continued to pray.

Please, Johanna, I beg of you, be there waiting for me. This death will be a blessing if only I can look once more into your soft, lovely eyes…

The hateful faces of the crowd dissolved into a gray blur. My eyes drifted upwards and I caught the flight of several black crows circling patiently overhead.

Johanna, always, I promise, always.

First the noises enveloping me disappeared. Then the pain. I found myself at peace and watched as the crows faded into blackness.

I know I died then. Nothing else would have been possible. So where was I? Purgatory? It had to be that. How could it be anything other than that? I couldn't move. I couldn't feel. I couldn't see. Utter despair filled my being. If I were in Purgatory how would I ever see my beloved Johanna again? But then as if to calm my fears a golden haze appeared before me and within it an image took shape. A face. My vision was too blurry for me to make out its details, but I knew it was a face. Of God? Who else could it be? As quickly as the despair had earlier come, so too now the joy and rapture that lifted me.

Words were spoken. The voice, though, was too soft for me to understand, and the words blurred together as if they were a hum intoned from far away.

And then I was in darkness again. Time crept intolerably slowly after that. It was agony as I waited to know what had happened to me. Worse even than what the executioner's skillful cudgel had been able to inflict. Was that truly the face of God I'd seen before? And if it was, would I be reunited with my Johanna, or was I to spend eternity in Purgatory, or worse?

My agony was suspended when once again the golden light filled my vision, and once again I was able to make out a face within its hazy glow, this time its features more distinct. The face appeared angelic, and my heart soared. And once more a voice spoke to me. While severely muffled, as if the speaker were underwater, I could make out the words.

"How are we now, my magnificent creation? Still unable to move? Not to worry. That will pass as you grow stronger. You can see me, can you? Oh how I wish you could answer me!"

Although his words confused me, his angelic countenance soothed my fears. If I were indeed in Purgatory, I would not be there for long. Darkness came quickly again, but this time I did not despair, although the loneliness I suffered had a heaviness to it that made me feel as if I were drowning. I concentrated to break this loneliness by picturing Johanna. Her soft hazel eyes, the rosiness of her cheeks, her golden flowing hair, the way her face would light up when she smiled at me. I tried to remember the way her hand fitted so perfectly in mine as we would walk along the woods outside of town, and the warmth against my lips when I would steal a kiss from her cheek.

Something strange happened while I pictured my Johanna. I once again saw the same yellowish glow from before, but this time it was because I realized I had developed the strength to open my eyes. I let my eyes close and once again I descended into darkness. I forced my eyes open and once more saw the glow.

I had believed the angelic face that earlier had appeared and the darkness that followed were caused by heavenly forces, but I realized that instead my eyelids earlier had been forcibly opened. That was why I saw that face peering into mine. It was only a man who had pushed my eyelids open, not God giving me a vision.

As this knowledge became irrefutable within my mind, a horrible dread seized me. I had survived the executioner's wheel. I wasn't in Purgatory, but instead still of this world. My body presumably lay wherever my host had brought me. Of course my body must be completely broken. But how was that possible? The executioner had shattered my bones, and yet I felt nothing. I knew the reason for this. My spine must have been broken as well as my limbs, so I could open my eyes, but otherwise I was in a state of paralysis. But still, it made no sense. It was not possible to survive the injuries that the executioner had inflicted on me. I was a chemist, a man of science, and I understood that as well as anyone. And yet I was alive.

The glow that I had believed was the breath of God was in fact sunlight filtering in through a window. I struggled to keep my eyes open, and when the room later fell into darkness, I knew it was because night had arrived.

My host returned again that night. From the faint flickers of light that showed, I surmised that he had lighted candles and had placed them around me. My senses were growing stronger for although the odor was faint to me, I could smell something foul and wretched. Possibly it was a salve that my host had placed over my wounds. As a chemist I was familiar with many compounds and I tried to detect what this one could have been made from, but the odor came from substances I was unfamiliar with. While I tried to solve this vexing puzzle, I heard my host chanting. His voice was too low for me to understand his words or even the language being used, but the rhythmic chanting felt as if it were something thick and oppressive. There was something unholy about it.

After the candles were snuffed out and my host had departed, I understood the truth. That I was in the dwelling of a sorcerer.

Chapter 2

I last saw Johanna the Sunday before my execution. She was the niece of my employer, Herr Klemmen, who owned the Ingolstadt apothecary where I was employed as a chemist. The beautiful Johanna was originally from Leipzig, but both her parents had died tragically from scarlet fever and she was sent to live with her uncle. From the first moment I saw her I was enraptured, and from the way she had blushed, as well as the smile that had escaped onto her lips, I knew that to some degree she shared my feelings. It wasn't long after our introduction that I began to court her, and with Herr Klemmen's blessing, Johanna consented to marry me.

Johanna and I shared so many of the same sentiments that are important for a joyful union. On most Sundays I would rent a carriage so that we could take it outside the city's walls and to the woods beyond. There we would walk along a path that I had discovered years earlier when I had first arrived in Ingolstadt. During our walks together we would collect wildflowers, mushrooms, and berries and enjoy the pleasant sights and sounds of nature. That last Sunday the gates to the city were to be locked and not to be opened until the next morning, so instead we strolled arm and arm through the main avenue of Ingolstadt, and I knew I was the envy of every young man who spied upon us. When we reached a grassy knoll near the city hall, I spread a blanket that I had brought, and Johanna and I sat together and talked about our upcoming wedding and the life that we were to share. I don't know if I ever knew more happiness than I did that afternoon. When I turned to steal a kiss, Johanna anticipated my intended theft and moved so that my lips pressed against her own instead of her cheek. She blushed deeply from this, but stayed positioned as she was so that our kiss would continue. A fever overtook me as our lips touched, and it was I who pulled away, afraid that I would burn up with ecstasy if I didn't.

After that we sat together quietly with her small delicate hand resting on top of my much coarser and larger hand. It was Johanna who spoke first, sighing with melancholy, and saying how she wished our wedding day had already come so that we wouldn't have to separate later. When I brought her back to Herr Klemmen's home, little could I have suspected that those would be our last moments together.

The next day started off ordinary enough. I woke at six, and performed my duties at the apothecary as usual from seven in the morning until seven that same evening. Once I left work, I stopped at the beer hall. This had been my custom, to relax and have a single pint of ale after my day's labor. But as I walked from the beer hall, a great and unexplained tiredness overtook me. I must have lain down in an alley to rest, though I don't remember doing it. My next memory was that of being violently awoken by a mob that had surrounded me. They demanded to know why I was sleeping in an alley, and as I struggled to come up with an explanation, one of them pointed toward my coat and exclaimed that it had my victim's blood marked upon it. With a great surprise I saw that the sleeves of my coat were stained with blood, and I could not answer where the blood had come from or how it had come to happen. They held me down and searched my person before pulling a gold locket from out of my trouser pocket.

"Why do you have this?" one of them demanded.

The locket was held in front of my eyes and I recognized it as belonging to Johanna. Inside the locket was a cameo of her beloved mother that had been carved in ivory. Johanna always wore that locket around her neck.

"I do not know," I said, too confused to understand the events that were transpiring, or the evil meaning of them. I couldn't fathom why I would have Johanna's prized locket in my possession, or why that fact would inspire such belligerence and hatred among this mob.

The one who held the locket opened it. When he saw the cameo within it he proclaimed me a murderer. I was still too confused to understand what he meant or to offer any defense of my innocence. The other members of the mob descended on me with their fists and beat me into near senselessness. I was then dragged to the city's jail, where I was locked behind iron bars.

Of course, I should have pieced together from what had happened that my dear Johanna had been cruelly murdered and that I was being accused as the fiend responsible, but my mind stayed lost in a cloud of confusion and refused to accept any of this. While I felt a sickening dread sinking into my heart, my mind worked to keep me in ignorance; otherwise the horror of the events would surely have crushed me.

The judge arrived at the jail a short time later, and I was brought out. The rest of the mob charged in behind me and filled up the room. I had heard stories of this judge, of course, but this was the first time I had been within his company. He was every bit as compassionless and stern as his reputation. A short and stout man of sixty with a harsh pallor to match his gray hair, he had the unnerving eyes of a bird of prey, and his features were likewise as sharp as a hawk's. I looked away from him and saw Herr Klemmen, but there was no love or compassion in his face either, and as he looked at me he trembled with rage. He only looked away when he was shown Johanna's locket. He confirmed in a choked voice that the locket had belonged to his niece.

The judge addressed me next. In a voice every bit as harsh as his features, he told me that the evidence against me was insurmountable. That with my victim's blood on my coat sleeves and her locket found in my trouser pocket, as well as the unexplained nature of my being found asleep in an alley, I had, without doubt, ravaged and murdered Johanna Klemmen.

It was only then that the fog surrounding my brain lifted and I could no longer deny what was evident. I fell to my knees sobbing. The thought of my Johanna being robbed of her life sank me into the deepest misery the human heart could know.

"Please, let me see my dearest Johanna," I begged through my weeping.

The judge scoffed at that. "You wish to view the fruits of your villainous act?" he asked in a voice bitter with outrage. "Herr Hoffmann, I find you one of the world's most contemptible creatures, and you will be shown the same mercy that you showed your betrothed, Johanna Klemmen. You are to be broken at the wheel in such a fashion as to cause the greatest amount of suffering. The executioner is commanded to wring every drop possible from your wretched body."

The crowd enthusiastically cheered the judge's decision. I couldn't speak. I had little concern for my own fate, and instead was too overwhelmed with what had befallen my beloved to utter a single word in my defense. They took me quickly from the jail to the courtyard beyond. The executioner's wheel sat there beckoning.

—⳾⳾⳾—

Sleep did not come to me that night, and my eyes had remained open to witness the first morning light that seeped into the room. The only physical movements available to me were the opening and closing of my eyes, but my senses seemed sharper. I could hear birds singing from outside, and as sunlight spread throughout the room my vision was no longer filled with a golden haziness, but instead I could now make out distinct patterns within the wood beam ceiling above me. All of this left no question that I was still of this earth. A body as shattered as mine should have fallen into death within hours, if not minutes. All I could imagine was that my host was indeed a sorcerer and had bewitched me. I had never before believed in witchcraft or spells, always attributing the stories I would hear to that of an uneducated and superstitious mind, but what else could explain my still being alive? The words of my host also troubled me. What could he have meant by calling me his *magnificent creature*? And his promise that in time I would grow stronger? My body had been left in an utterly ruined state. Unless magic was to be used to repair my body, that would not be possible. There was nothing known within the scientific world that could undo the damage that had been done to me.

Later that morning my host arrived. At least I believed it was still morning, for I had difficulty in my present state judging the passing of time. But it seemed as if only a few hours had passed since those first morning rays of sunlight appeared before I heard a door opening, and then footsteps creaking along a wooden floor. While I couldn't see him, I recognized his voice when he called out to remark how glad he was that I was now able to open my eyes.

"Good, good," he exclaimed with much excitement, "this means that you are becoming stronger, my pet!"

His voice sounded familiar, and not just because I had heard him the other day. Somewhere in my past I had heard his voice before. When my host sat beside me and leaned over me to peer into my face, I could see his own face clearly. The other day where I saw a hazy blur I now saw well-defined features. His was a youthful but serious face, a face that

many would judge as handsome. Thin with a high forehead
and a Roman nose. His lips were full and his eyes held a
piercing quality. But it wasn't an angelic face as I had first
deluded myself the other day. There was a falseness to the
smile that he bestowed upon me, and his eyes while sharp
and intelligent had a cruelty to them. As I had recognized his
voice, so I also did his face. He had been a customer of the
apothecary, and there were several occasions when we had
conversed. His purpose at the apothecary had always been
to buy compounds for his studies, being that he was a student
at the University. From our conversations, I remembered that
his field of study was medicine, and at one time we had discussed advances in chemistry at length. With a great effort
of concentration I recalled his name. Victor Frankenstein.

He moved his face very close to mine and stayed positioned that way for a long moment before straightening in
his seat.

"Your eyes are still very watery," he said, "but your
pupils are more defined, less dilated. I would venture to say
that you can see far more clearly today, my pet. I would also
guess that your sense of hearing must likewise be improving,
but for what purpose? What could you possibly make of my
words? To you they must sound as the same garbled noises
that any newborn would hear. A pity."

Once again I was greatly confused. Frankenstein suspected that my hearing was improving, so he would have
known I wasn't deaf. So why would he believe that I would
be incapable of understanding his words? We had conversed
before, he must have remembered that. Did he think that my
injuries had left me unable to understand my own native language? I tried to call out to him for I badly desired to ask him
those questions and many more, but I remained mute, for I
lacked the strength even to open my mouth.

Frankenstein left his seat. His presence remained near to

me, and I presumed he had set about to vigorously rub life back into my deadened limbs. This was a presumption on my part, for while some of my senses were returning, my skin remained devoid of sensation. Occasionally he would enter my field of vision and that appeared to me to be the activity that he was engaged in.

While this went on I thought about what had occurred the night before. Maybe I was mistaken. How could I trust my perceptions with everything that has happened? What I thought had been satanic chanting could have been nothing more than hallucinations, perhaps even brought on by the foul-smelling balm that he had applied to my person. Frankenstein was a medical student, a man of science like myself; perhaps during his studies he had discovered a new procedure to restore health to a body as broken as mine. And while I prided myself on being familiar with all materials known to an apothecary, that strange balm that he used could have been a new discovery of his instead of something unholy as I had imagined. As these thoughts consumed me, I felt a great anger that he had interfered with my dying; for by keeping me constrained within the earthly plane he was robbing me of being reunited with my Johanna within the kingdom of Heaven. Eventually, though, I realized that if Frankenstein could truly bring me back to health, then I would have the opportunity to discover and expose Johanna's murderer and seek justice for my beloved. While my additional days on earth without her company would be torturous, eventually those would pass, and when we were eventually joined it would be with the knowledge that this terrible crime committed upon her had been avenged.

My thoughts were interrupted by a dizzying sensation as the room moved on me, and I realized that the table I was lying on was being tilted upwards by a hand crank so that I would be in a more upright position.

"This should help keep your blood from congealing," Frankenstein said, his voice strained from his exertion. He giggled in a mad sort of way that chilled my blood. "Besides," he added with a sly overtone, "I am sure you must desire the company of the fairer sex."

Before my eyes lay a severed head. I squeezed my eyes closed, not believing what I had seen, maybe even thinking it could have been an apparition, but when I opened them again the head was still there. The head was that from a woman. She had perhaps been beautiful when she was alive, but there was now a horrible gauntness to her features, the cheeks hollowed, the eyes sunk deep within the flesh, only wisps of brownish hair still remaining on its scalp. The skin was grayish in color and had the appearance of parchment paper, and from the way the mouth pushed inwards it gave the impression that the teeth had been removed. The severed head sat in a bowl, positioned so that it was facing me, a short stump of its neck still attached. A milky substance that was about two inches deep filled the bottom of the bowl. For a long moment I stared, transfixed. Then, seemingly, it came alive and its eyes shifted to lock onto mine. I would have screamed if I could have.

Frankenstein giggled some more. "I'll leave you, my pet, to become better acquainted with our dear Sophie." He walked over to the shelf that the severed head had been placed on and caressed the scalp as if he were caressing a small dog. Frankenstein turned to smile cruelly at me, and then he disappeared from my field of vision. Shortly after that there was further creaking of footsteps along the floor and the sound of a door being pulled closed.

I squeezed my eyes shut once more and prayed that this severed head would be gone when I opened my eyes again, but not only was it still facing me with its eyes staring vigilantly into mine, but its lips had begun moving. My earlier suspicions proved correct. As that awful gaping hole contorted wildly in front of me, I could not help but notice that it was bereft of its teeth.

What additional horrors could possibly befall me? Any thoughts that I was being kept alive by scientific means fled my consciousness. There was no longer any doubt that I had woken up in the den of a sorcerer and that the blackest magic was being practiced.

I shut my eyes again, but the image within my mind of what this severed head was presently doing grew worse than what it could possibly be in reality. I had no choice but to look straight ahead and face it. As I did I realized that the movements of its lips weren't the result of random contortions, but that it was trying to mouth words to me, her language being French which I understood. I concentrated and was able to make out what she was trying to say.

Blink once if you can understand me.

I blinked once.

A tragic smile touched her lips and her eyes overflowed with compassion. What I had earlier thought of as a wretched thing I now felt sympathy toward. She began to ask me another question, her lips moving slowly and carefully to make it easier for me to understand her.

Are you able to speak? Please blink once for yes, twice for no.

I blinked twice.

Her smile turned ever more tragic. She began once again to mouth words to me.

My dear unfortunate friend, my name is not Sophie. It is Charlotte, but that is of no importance. If you regain your ability to speak, you must not do so, at least not in his presence.

She explained that our host believed us to be imbecilic and that it would be extremely dangerous for us if he learned of our intelligence. She further detailed her sad history to me. She had been married to a soldier and was living in Paris when she became tragically widowed. In order to support herself, she became employed as a seamstress. When she lost her employment she had to resort to begging. One Sunday a man whom she believed to be a libertine asked her if she would like to earn money as a chambermaid. While she was suspicious of his true intentions, she was desperate and accepted his offer. He took her to a grand house in the community of Arcueil, which was only a few miles from the center of Paris. Once there, he insisted that they each drink a glass of cognac, and that she drink hers first. She consented, and shortly afterward she became unnaturally tired, and most likely collapsed to the floor unconscious. When she later awoke she found herself in this wretched nightmare. Now all she could do was pray that her nightmare would end and that she be released fully into death.

It was a heart-wrenching story, and I could feel nothing but the deepest sympathy toward her. At the completion of her tale, her expression suddenly became dull. I was so engrossed in her tale that I failed to notice that our host had returned. Fortunately, Charlotte had.

"Ah, my dear pet, I believe you have been in this upright position long enough. It won't do to have all your blood flowing to your feet."

He came into view. A curious look showed on his face as he studied me, and he took a silk handkerchief from his pocket to dab at my face. "Your eyes are so watery," he said. "Some of it has been spilling down your cheeks."

After he finished with his dabbing, he used the hand crank to lower the table to a horizontal position, and Charlotte disappeared from my view. Of course I knew I had been drugged when I had visited the beer hall, and when I heard Charlotte's story of how she had been drugged inside of the house that she had been brought to, I knew we were both victims of the same fiend, our host, Victor Frankenstein.

At the same time that I had lain drugged in that alley, my beloved Johanna must have been brutally murdered, her blood used to stain my coat sleeves and her locket placed within my trouser pocket. Just as Frankenstein had made Charlotte the victim of a depraved experiment, so must he have similar designs for me. Why, I did not know, but I would have given anything to have enough strength in my hands so that I could force the truth from Frankenstein. But I was defenseless and at his mercy.

CHAPTER 3

Four days passed with Frankenstein each night making his unholy visit. First he would apply his foul ointment upon my body, next he would light candles and place them on the floor below me so that they would surround me. After that had been accomplished he would sit nearby and chant in that same evil low voice that he had that first night. While I was unable to decipher his words, they nonetheless chilled my soul.

It was on the fifth day that he raised me vertically so I would once again be in Charlotte's company. After Frankenstein had used the hand crank to put me at eye level with Charlotte, he smiled thinly and remarked how we made quite the adorable couple.

Once Frankenstein departed, Charlotte regaled me with happier tales from her life. As she was telling me about a particularly joyous day from her childhood, she stopped to announce in her silent manner that I was smiling.

Only the barest trace of a smile, my dearest friend, but you are smiling nonetheless.

She was right. Without realizing it the corners of my lips had turned up ever so slightly. With a concentrated effort I found that I could move my lips. Not enough to speak, or even to mouth words as Charlotte was doing, but I had movement now where only a day earlier I had none.

Charlotte was smiling at me also, but a darkness descended over her features and she cast her eyes downwards before looking up to meet my own eyes again.

When he lights his candles each night, there are five of

*them. I believe he places them on the floor to form the shape
of a pentagram.*

I had suspected that also. The Devil's hoofprint.

The sound of a door opening interrupted us, and from
the way Charlotte's expression deadened I knew that our host
had returned. His footsteps made a dull hollow sound as he
entered the room. When he came into my field of vision I
could see that same false smile of his that I had grown to
know and detest.

"Ah, my pet," he said with utter condescension, "one
should hope that you haven't been too forward with our
dearest Sophie, for I assure you she is of the highest virtue."

He broke into a giggling fit after that, which ended only
due to his exertion in turning the hand crank to lower me.
Once I was lowered back into a horizontal position, he stood
looking over me with a gleam of perspiration along his forehead. He sniffed several times. His smile disappeared as his
eyes bored into mine.

"There appears to be a problem. But perhaps we will be
able to catch it in time."

I also recognized the stench that he had detected. The
smell of decaying flesh. I had noticed it earlier. It was faint,
but still present. Frankenstein next began to poke his finger
along my body. I knew this for I was beginning to develop a
finer sensation along my skin.

"Ah, the source of the trouble," he murmured softly.
"Well, let us give it time and see if we can reverse this."

He was out of my field of vision so I could not see
where his stare was fixed upon. I had the sense that it was
my left arm that showed signs of decay, but if he had poked
me there I didn't feel it. This change did seem to create a
more somber expression upon Frankenstein's visage. When
I spied him next, his brow had become deeply lined, and an
anxiousness pulled at the corners of his lips. He left the

room without another word, seemingly deep in thought.

That night Frankenstein returned to perform his usual nocturnal rituals. By morning the stench of flesh decaying had grown more obvious. When Frankenstein appeared, concern lined his face. I was ambivalent. While I wished for the opportunity to grow stronger so that I might force the truth from him regarding myself and Johanna, I also welcomed the release that death would give me. From out of the corner of my eye I could see Frankenstein's expression growing ever more troubled as he examined me. He was brooding as he walked away. When he appeared again a short time later he held a saw. Without so much as a word he went to work.

While the sensation was dulled, I felt the saw blade biting into my flesh. Frankenstein was cutting my left arm off directly below the shoulder blade. It seemed to take a great effort on his part, as well as quite a long time. During it I felt little pain, not much more than a tugging sensation. When he was done I caught a glimpse of the appendage that he had severed, and I could hardly believe what I saw. It was something monstrous, both in size and appearance. How could that have come from my body? Gnarled and muscular, with dark black hair growing in clumps along it. Other than the unearthly translucence of the flesh, it seemed more of what would've been cut off from a giant ape than any human being. The knowledge that that came from me stunned me and sent me spiraling into a deep despair. I was barely aware when Frankenstein departed, carrying away that unearthly appendage.

Up until then I had assumed that Frankenstein was using his dark arts to repair my paralyzed and badly broken body, but how could that still be the case? Unless I only imagined what I saw. After all, wouldn't having my arm cut from me as if it were only a limb from a tree leave me in a state of shock? How could I trust my senses after that? Perhaps I had long ago fallen into madness and everything that I believed I was perceiving was only a nightmarish illusion. Charlotte, Frankenstein's nocturnal visits, the ungodly appendage taken from my body. I wished to believe that. If I was insane then none of this would be true. I tried to hold onto that belief, but doubt slowly wormed its way into my thoughts, and as hellish as these events were I had to believe them to be true.

So what was I then? Was my previous body taken away to be replaced by something hideous? How? A horrible thought entered my mind. Did Frankenstein somehow trap my spirit into some sort of unearthly creation of his? That arm could not have come from any known animal in nature. Frankenstein's evil words came back to me. *My magnificent creation.* Was that what I was? A creation of his? An even more horrible thought occurred to me. Could I trust my sense of self? If I were truly an unearthly being that he created, was it possible that my memories were only imagined? Could it be that Johanna never truly existed?

If I could have I would have roared in agony. But I lacked the strength to do so. All I could do was lie where I was. I lacked even the strength to weep.

CHAPTER 4

My host maintained his nocturnal rituals. It was three days after Frankenstein had cut off my arm that he came to me to sew a new appendage to my body. A glimpse that I caught of it showed it to be of a similar nature to what had been removed. By this time I had more movement than I had had previously. I could open my mouth enough where I would be able to mouth words to Charlotte if given the opportunity. I could also move my fingers slightly on my remaining hand. I kept this from Frankenstein. I did not want to let him in on the knowledge that I was gaining strength, as feeble as my progress appeared. I further restrained myself from showing any change in facial expression as Frankenstein performed his sewing.

"Almost done, my pet," Frankenstein grunted as he tugged at the thread. "I do so regret the delay, but obtaining the necessary material was not easy, nor was the labor necessary to build you this new arm. But I do expect it to be as functional as the one I needed to remove. We will see."

When he was done he applied more of that foul-smelling balm along the area that had been stitched.

"This will set us back, of course," Frankenstein muttered, as if to himself. "A pity. But let us hope this new arm will take. In the meantime, your blood has remained stagnant for too long and we need to get it moving again."

He used the hand crank to raise me. After he left, I surprised Charlotte by mouthing words to her.

What am I?

A sadness pervaded Charlotte's features as she realized

what I was asking. She attempted a fragile smile toward me.

You are a gentle soul. I can read that much from your eyes.

But what of my appearance? What am I outwardly?

I do not know.

I begged Charlotte to describe me. Pain squeezed her features for a moment, but then she attempted a whimsical smile.

You were missing an arm. That has been replaced. But myself, am I not missing a whole body?

Please, Charlotte, I beg of you. How do I appear?

You are very large. Let us leave it at that, and please do not make me say any more. Tell me instead of happier days from your life so that both our spirits may be lifted.

I relented and did not press Charlotte further for details. I told her of how when I first saw my Johanna I was completely enraptured by her beauty, and later how nervous I was when I attempted to work up the courage to first ask her to join me on a Sunday stroll and how my spirit soared when she said yes. I tried to maintain a happy countenance as I related my history to Charlotte, but I was deeply troubled, for how could I trust my memories after the lunacy I had fallen into? The image that I carried of myself was of a man of fair complexion and slight build. That grotesque appendage taken from my body shattered this image. If my body was that of a monstrous creature, then how could I believe my other memories to be true? From words Frankenstein had spoken earlier, he seemed to be of the belief that he created me. If that were true then maybe he had also created the memories contained within me that now seemed so dear. Was it possible that I, Friedrich Hoffmann, never actually existed? And if that were so, is it further possible that my beloved Johanna was also nothing but a figment of my imagination? It was both horrible and joyous to think that that could be the case. Horrible to think that a being as wonderful as my Johanna was never really a part of this world, and that the love and passion that I was so sure I felt toward her was only imaginary. But it was joyous to think that if all this was purely illusionary then the sweet Johanna that existed within my memories never had to suffer the cruel fate that I imagined had befallen her.

I was so caught up in my thoughts that I failed to notice Charlotte's expression dimming or the door being opened, and was in the midst of relating a story to Charlotte when Frankenstein appeared in my peripheral vision. Terror filled me with the thought that I had betrayed my secret knowledge to him, and worse, betrayed Charlotte's confidence, but when Frankenstein laughed out loud I realized that wasn't the case.

"Ah, my dear pet," he exclaimed happily. "You now have the ability to use your jaw muscles. How wonderful! But what are you trying to do to Sophie? Eat her? She is not food, my pet! Or am I mistaken? Are you so bewitched by her beauty that you are trying to enjoy her carnally? I am afraid that too great a distance separates you both for your lips to reach, at least not without my help!"

Frankenstein giggled to himself, and when he picked up the bowl that Charlotte's head rested in I thought he was going to bring her to me to force our lips to press. Instead, though, he smiled mockingly at me and placed his index finger on her lips for her to suckle on, all the while giggling in that insidious manner of his. Oh how I despised him and wished that I had regained enough strength to throttle him! But even as I burned in my hatred I was relieved that he had failed to divine the true nature of what he had seen.

Frankenstein's giggling ceased. A hardness showed in his eyes as he placed Charlotte on her shelf. Then he turned those cruel eyes toward me, studying me as if I were little more than an insect under a piece of glass.

"If you have the strength to move your jaw muscle, I wonder what other strength you have recovered? Can you not yet move your fingers, your toes?" he mused softly. "More importantly, I must wonder why you are hiding this from me? Is it simply an animal cunning that has taken over?"

He pursed his lips as he continued his black-hearted study of me. During it I fought to keep my expression empty so that I might hide my intelligence from him. At last he gave up.

"Is it that my presence simply leaves you paralyzed with fear, the same as a fox may leave a rabbit?" he queried. "Whatever the reason, it doesn't matter. What does matter is that you are regaining your strength, and with luck this new arm that I have crafted will grow to be part of you. And perhaps enough intelligence will develop in your brain so that someday I may learn the truth regarding this curious behavior of yours. We shall see."

Frankenstein proceeded to lower me once more. Shortly after he left I heard a low but horrible bellowing noise, as if made by a wild animal with its leg caught in a trap. Only after I later felt a sensation of wetness upon my cheeks did I understand that I was the source of this terrible noise. It was the sound of my own weeping.

CHAPTER 5

I became familiar with a routine. A dreary and mostly hellish routine. No matter what the human spirit may be confronted with, we appear to possess the capacity for settling into habits so that we may be able to survive our circumstances, no matter how horrific they may be. After seeing the appendage that was removed from me, I had to confront the fact that my being was something other than that of a man, but still, I stubbornly believed my spirit and sentiments to be human.

Each night Frankenstein would perform his ungodly rituals. During the day I was mostly left alone to contemplate the horrors that had befallen me, with my only respite being when every third day or so I would be raised to a more vertical position. The reason for this, according to my host, was to keep my blood from settling and more rot from occurring, although I suspected Frankenstein also took perverse pleasure in having Charlotte and I face each other. Little could he have suspected that I greatly welcomed the company of Charlotte a fellow creature made equally as miserable as myself. During these brief respites we would converse in our silent manner. While I desperately wished to know what I had become, I made no attempt to extract from her the nature of my appearance. Mostly from Charlotte I received the warmth of human compassion, which was completely absent from Frankenstein, who radiated nothing but mockery and cruelty.

The appendage that Frankenstein manufactured to

replace the one that had decayed successfully attached itself
to my body. As the days passed, my strength grew, although
what I had was still very little. I did however gain the power
to move my neck sufficiently to see more of my surroundings. The room I had been placed in appeared to be a laboratory, with both familiar and unfamiliar medical apparatus
cluttering several tables. Enough sensation had also returned
to my skin so that I determined that a fabric had been lain
across my body. My appearance was still mostly a mystery to
me. I lacked even the strength to lift my hands to the necessary height so that I could view them.

Not once did I sleep. Perhaps this inability was due to
Frankenstein's nightly satanic chanting. Or perhaps sleep
was simply a component missing from the form of creature
that I resided within. Or it could be simply that my lack of
physical activity left me with no compulsion to sleep. There
were other normal bodily functions that were absent within
me, most noticeably that I did not receive any nourishment
or liquids. I wondered about that, for every known species
of creature requires nourishment and water to survive, and
I had had neither for over forty days. I suspected that the
foul ointment Frankenstein applied to me nightly had been
seeping into my body and, in some ungodly way, was providing me the nourishment that food and water would normally give.

As the days passed, Frankenstein's demeanor grew de-
cisively excited. He scurried about his laboratory, his
cheeks flushing a bright pink, all the while remarking that
we were soon to be visited by an honored guest. It was late
one afternoon when I heard Frankenstein's voice drifting
in from outside of the room, and soon realized he was conversing in French with another man. The two of them must
have been in a room adjacent to the one that I was housed
in, and I could hear them without much strain through the

walls. At first the two men exchanged pleasantries with Frankenstein addressing this other man as "my dear Marquis." He spoke with a reverence and subservience that seemed unnatural for him. After Frankenstein had expressed his hope that this other man had enjoyed a comfortable journey, his voice nearly tittered in excitement as he commented on the notorious stories he had heard over the years concerning a Rose Keller.

"Bah!" this other man exclaimed angrily. "They made it out as if I had slaughtered and dismembered a roomful of wenches instead of merely flogging the ass of one particularly opportunistic whore! And the way they treated me. A nobleman. All because of a few welts on the backside of a whore? Enough of that. Victor, must you keep me in suspense much longer? I have been anticipating this creation of yours ever since we began our correspondences and you proposed the idea to me."

"I will be keeping you in suspense a while longer for I have another surprise for you. Really only a novelty, but one that I believe you will find of interest."

The door to the laboratory opened and Frankenstein entered moving in an excited pace. I dared to lift my head high enough to spot him, but he was too eager in his intentions to notice. Near breathless, he raced to where Charlotte rested and took hold of the bowl that she was within. He exited the room while carrying the bowl in one hand and stroking her scalp with his other. From beyond I heard this other man, this Marquis, shout out in surprise.

"Its eyes! They're moving! Does it possess intelligence?"

"Sadly, no. She is little more than an amusement. But watch how she suckles my finger when I place it near her mouth."

There were several moments of quiet, then the Marquis shouting out again.

"How . . . how do you explain this?"

Frankenstein hesitated before explaining, "My dear Sophie was a whore when she was alive. From Paris. I believe what she is doing now is mimicking behavior that still remains ingrained deep within the recesses of her brain."

"A Parisian whore, you say? I have been intimate with so many, but I must have missed this one while I was locked away in the Bastille. Why the milky liquid in the bowl?"

"That is how she receives nourishment, by absorbing the liquid through the bottom of her neck. Think of her as an orchid growing in a pot."

"Fascinating, truly fascinating. Can it exist outside of the bowl?"

"For several hours, yes. After that she would wilt and die."

"I see that you have taken the precaution of removing its teeth," the Marquis said. "My dear Victor, please do hand it to me. I desire to have it suckle my finger also."

My blood boiled as I heard the way they discussed Charlotte as if she were a plaything. During one of our visits together, Charlotte explained to me that it was better for her to lick Frankenstein's finger than for him to surmise the intelligence that she held. But her eyes also flashed with ferocity as she wished that she still had her teeth so that she would've been able to bite off whatever she could of his.

If I had had the power to do so I would have left the table that I was stranded on and crushed both their skulls. When I heard this despicable Marquis remark how he would later make use of Charlotte once he was properly rested from his traveling, I found myself choking with hatred toward this man as I understood his depraved intentions.

They must have grown tired of Charlotte, for the door to the laboratory opened and the creaking of footsteps entered into the room; one pair of footsteps that was heavy and slow, the other all too familiar. I lay on my back staring at the wood-beam ceiling above me. I did not want to give them the advantage of knowing that I had movement within my neck. A loud gasp escaped from the Marquis.

"My God! Is that actually alive?"

"Very much alive."

"Are . . . are we safe?"

"Oh yes. Even if he had the strength to rise we would be safe. But for now the creature barely has the ability to raise his hands several inches from the table. Interestingly, he tries to hide this from me. Some sort of animal cunning, I suppose."

Footsteps approached. The Marquis turned out to be a short and rotund man of about fifty. He was almost entirely bald, his features having a grayish, unhealthy tinge to them and his round, fleshy face seeming almost a caricature of a man who had once been thin and handsome. Timidly, he peered over me, his face awash with fear and curiosity, but even still, a haughtiness pervaded his eyes and lips.

"My God," the Marquis whispered. "To think that you made this. How?"

"A complicated process," Frankenstein said with an air of smugness. "The limbs and trunk and head were all fashioned from materials that I had collected, but these would have been of little use without the secret books of alchemy and dark arts that I was most fortunate to have uncovered. Without these volumes, none of this would be possible."

Fear slowly abated from the Marquis's pale eyes. He leaned in closer to me, his breath warm upon me.

"Do not dare to tell me there is not intelligence in those eyes!" the Marquis claimed. "I swear he understands every word we speak!"

Frankenstein laughed at that. "My dear Marquis," he said, "I do not wish to contradict you, but no, that is not the case. His intelligence would be little more than what you could expect from a four-month-old infant. For now, that is all there is. There exists no knowledge within him, and certainly no understanding of language."

"But I can see the brightness in those horrible watery eyes!"

"Animal cunning, that is all. The brain was obtained from an educated man. The capability of intelligence exists, and with enough schooling this creature could perhaps develop the art of language, but that would require years, if it were indeed possible."

The Marquis disappeared from view. In my mind's eye I could imagine him stroking his chin that was so deeply buried in flesh, his brow worried as if he were profoundly deep in thought. The image of this ridiculous little man in such a state struck me as comical and I must have smiled without realizing it for the Marquis exclaimed with excitement, "Victor, look at how a grin wrinkles its face!"

"Do not newborn infants also grin mysteriously?" Frankenstein asked.

The Marquis made a soft humming noise as he considered this. In the end he accepted Frankenstein's explanation and asked him to remove the blanket from my body. I felt the fabric pulled from me. At the same moment a gasping sound emanated from the Marquis.

"This abomination of yours," the Marquis sputtered, his voice strangled. "It is magnificently horrific, far surpassing what I had imagined. Look at the sex organ that you constructed for it! It would be the envy of many a stallion! Perhaps there is even enough there to satisfy that empress of Russia! Does it function? Please do tell me that it does!"

"An interesting question, my dear Marquis, and one that I am also curious about. For now, no, there is not yet enough strength in the creature for such activity. But in the future? I do not know. Time will tell."

"If it does . . . if it does . . ." the Marquis's voice broke off. A brief moment later he continued, his voice having grown exceedingly heated. "Oh, if it does function we would be able to bring more than my masterpiece to life. This creature . . . this is how I have been envisioning a grotesque giant that I will be naming Minski for a novel that I am currently involved in writing and which will carry the simple title, *Juliette*. Later I must share these details with you. When I do you will also see how with your magnificent creature we will also be able to create a living tribute to this novel, as well as my masterpiece. I have goose bumps, Victor, simply imagining it."

Frankenstein and the Marquis continued their heated conversation but it mostly turned into a droning noise in my ears. I would catch pieces of what they would say; the Marquis bitterly complaining about a number of issues: his financial situation, his mother-in-law and her attempts to ruin his life, and how he wept tears of blood when his masterpiece was lost in the Bastille, while Frankenstein eagerly entreated the Marquis to describe his latest novel. It was difficult for me to pay much attention to them. Mostly my thoughts kept returning back to Frankenstein's earlier words: *the brain was obtained from an educated man.*

During the many days that I had been housed in Frankenstein's laboratory, I heard frequent comments uttered from him about how I had been created from materials. I had also seen evidence to support his claims, making it impossible to have believed otherwise. I had begun to suspect that the memories I held so dear were merely illusions. But if Frankenstein had acquired the brain of an educated man to create me, could that man have been Friedrich Hoffmann? Could that be why I believed so dearly that I was this same man? If these memories were real, and if that was the reason I was convinced that I was Friedrich Hoffmann, did that not make me Friedrich Hoffmann, even if other materials were used to construct my body? And what of my soul? How could I possibly have one if I were simply a collection of materials joined together? Charlotte claimed that she could see my soul in my eyes and that it was a gentle one. How could that be? Was it possible that my soul, or should I say, Friedrich Hoffmann's soul, entered this manufactured body? Or was I in fact soulless, a creature brought into this world through satanic magic? How could such a creature possess a soul?

These thoughts and other metaphysical questions that they raised troubled me greatly, as did the idea that Frankenstein executed the murder of the woman I believed to be my beloved Johanna for the sole purpose of arranging to have Friedrich Hoffmann blamed for her murder. And for what reason? Simply to gain access to an educated brain? The evil necessary to perpetrate such acts was more than I could fathom.

At some point Frankenstein had covered me again with the same fabric and he and his guest departed, but I wasn't aware of it until I noticed that the chill brought from his presence was gone and that the laboratory had become deathly quiet.

In the end I decided that my memories and sentiments, if they were indeed real, would make me Friedrich Hoffmann regardless of the body that I now resided in. I would trust Charlotte that she did indeed see a gentle soul within me. Even if the darkest satanic magic was used to bring me to life, that did not have to mean that I was an instrument of the Devil, even if I was now consumed with evil desires, mainly the thoughts of murdering Frankenstein and his equally detestable Marquis.

CHAPTER 6

That same day the Marquis arrived, Frankenstein took Charlotte from the laboratory once night had fallen, and didn't return her to her shelf for several days. My heart sank in knowing the Marquis's sickening intentions, but I never asked Charlotte what had happened. I knew without asking her that she had suffered inhumanely, for whatever dim light had previously shone in her eyes had been extinguished upon her return. As it turned out we only had a few remaining respites to spend together. Even with the cruelty that she had been forced to endure, during our brief final minutes, Charlotte still tried with all her soul to raise my own beleaguered spirits.

The day after his arrival the Marquis performed a closer inspection of me, his breath heavy with cognac. A malignance shone in those awful, pale eyes of his as he ran his hands slowly across my body, touching me in unnatural ways. At first all I could do was imagine wrapping my hands around his throat and squeezing that insipid smile from his bloated face, but as I strained to do this my hands failed to lift more than several inches from the table. Finally I calmed myself by knowing that our situation would someday be reversed, and that he would be the one trembling under my touch.

Several days later the Marquis departed. From what I could tell from conversations that he held with Frankenstein within my presence, there were others involved in their enterprise, including a group of wealthy men who were chiefly providing financing. They talked in a mostly cryptic manner, however, and I was unable to learn more of their plans other than they envisioned me playing an important role.

Daily I was growing in strength. These improvements were slow but steady, and I dreamed that I would be able to surprise Frankenstein soon by taking hold of him and breaking his neck. Two weeks after the Marquis had left, Frankenstein thwarted my plans by tying leather straps around my body and securing me tightly to the table. Silently I cursed him for this, for I felt I was only days away from being able to rise from my imprisonment. While I had diligently tried to keep my growing strength from him, he somehow had surmised my improvement and the closeness of my revenge, and he took the proper precautions. The look he gave me as he tightened the straps around my body chilled me, as if he could read my very thoughts.

The very next day after he had strapped me to the table, he packed up his laboratory, emptying it of all of its contents, including Charlotte, so that only I remained. That night for the first time he failed to make his nocturnal visit.

I don't think I ever felt more alone than I did that next day when sunlight first crept into the room. I had a gnawing suspicion that Victor Frankenstein had left the premises for good, and that I would lie strapped upon that table until I either withered and died, or until some stranger discovered me and slaughtered me for being an ungodly creature. The cruelty of that was more than I could take, for if that were to happen I would never know if Friedrich Hoffmann and the dear woman whom I believed to have been my beloved truly existed or were merely figments of my imagination. And if my dear Johanna had existed, I would never have the opportunity to avenge her murder.

I wept silently then, and continued to weep until I was too exhausted for even that. Eventually night arrived, and I remained helpless and alone in that cursed room. That night, like every other night since Frankenstein brought me into the world, I lay awake without the hope of sleep to offer me a temporary reprieve from my misery.

A week passed without any change in my situation, except that I began to feel the slow gnawing of hunger and a horrible thirst, which confirmed my earlier thoughts about the ointment that Frankenstein had applied nightly to my body. The loneliness I felt was crushing. Even when Charlotte had been held outside of my view, I drew comfort knowing that a sympathetic soul resided only a few feet from me. The miserable nature of my new circumstances must have pushed me closer to madness, for I even found myself missing my host's nightly satanic chanting.

Frankenstein's abrupt departure and my abandonment made little sense, at least if I were truly as crucial to his plans as he and the Marquis had implied. What could possibly be the reason for these actions? A cold panic overtook me as I understood what must have happened. They had been discovered. That was the only explanation for these rash developments. Their fiendish plans had been discovered and they were now running for their lives.

A hopelessness welled up within me and I unleashed a horrible bellow, the coarseness and inhuman nature of the sound surprising me. I realized my cry might draw strangers to the dwelling and lead to my discovery, but I did not care. If strangers desired to slaughter me while I lay tied and helpless, I welcomed it. At least it would speed a possible reunion with Johanna, if she had in fact existed, and if Friedrich Hoffmann's soul resided in my body as I prayed it did. I bellowed until I was hoarse, but it brought no visitors.

Please God, I begged, end this.

Just as a hopelessness had only minutes earlier taken me over, so did now an all-consuming rage. How could a merciful God allow these atrocities? And if the spirit residing in me was human, and if I was being tested in my faith as Job had been, how could any God put one of his unfortunate children through the horrors that I had endured? If I were Friedrich Hoffmann as I believed, maybe I hadn't always been the most devout practitioner of faith, and maybe during my life I had leaned more toward science than the church, but I had always tried to live an honorable life. How could I have deserved this?

I bellowed again in rage, and stopped only when I realized the leather strap that had been tied around my chest had broken. The slow trickle of strength that had been ever so slowing ebbing back into my body must have turned into a raging torrent over the last few days, for in my rage I broke that strap, which was something not even a wild beast could have done. I sat up with ease and tore apart the strap that bound my legs to the table as easily as a child might have torn a paper ribbon.

I was free.

Clumsily, I fell to the floor, my legs feeling foreign to me. As I balanced on my feet and stood up, the top of my head brushed the very same wood-beam ceiling that I had spent so many hours staring at. What the Marquis had said was true. I was enormous in size, at least eight feet in height. For several moments I tottered on my feet before I gained my balance. With every breath I felt more strength in my legs, as if they were becoming more a part of me. I lifted my hands to my face and gasped at what I saw. As with the glimpse I had caught earlier of the rotted appendage that had been cut from me, these were monstrous hands. Large and gnarled, with that same unearthly translucent flesh, and matted black hair which grew out in clumps along my knuckles and even on my palms. But they were also strong and powerful. I could feel the strength in them as I squeezed them closed. I looked down at my legs and saw they were of the same nature.

Crouching so that my scalp didn't hit the ceiling, I left

the laboratory. The adjacent room appeared to be a sitting room. Like the laboratory it had been emptied. Beyond the sitting room was what must have been Frankenstein's living quarters. I went through these rooms carefully, hoping to find something that would indicate where Frankenstein had fled, but these rooms, outside of a few scattered objects of worn furniture, had been emptied also. A dressing mirror rested on the floor of what must have been Frankenstein's bedroom. Trepidation filled me as I crept toward the mirror. Nothing could have prepared me for the hideous apparition that looked back out at me as I bent low in front of the mirror. My face was that of a daemon. Twisted, distorted, the mouth an ugly knife-slit and the flesh that same strange grayish skin that covered my appendages and hands. A thing of nightmares. My eyes in particular were awful. Watery, and what in normal eyes are white, in mine a yellowish-bloody color. I could barely stand to look at myself, and I turned away from the mirror. I stood frozen for a long moment before searching the rest of Frankenstein's quarters, but found nothing that could help me.

When I was done I went back to the laboratory so that I could take the blanket that had earlier covered my body, and wrapped it around my middle. I then exited the doorway that led out of the apartment, and found myself at the top of a staircase. Frankenstein must have rented the top floor of a rooming house. Why no one came to investigate my earlier bellowing, I couldn't say. Perhaps Frankenstein had also rented the other floors so that he would have privacy, but I chose not to investigate. All I wanted to do was leave that cursed place. I bent low and made my way down that narrow staircase. The outer door led to an alley. I stepped outside and stood gasping in fresh air and feeling the sun's warm rays upon my face as I looked heavenward. Noises from the street beyond reminded me of my situation. I stole quietly down the alley and saw the bustle of men and women as they made their way down the street, and as I watched them I realized I couldn't leave this way, not without raising a mob against me. Instead I came up with another plan.

CHAPTER 7

I reentered Frankenstein's laboratory. From there I climbed out of a window and lifted myself onto the roof. The pitch of the roof was steep, but it gave me little trouble and I scrambled to the top while keeping my body low so that anyone glancing upwards wouldn't see me.

From my vantage point I could see several familiar sites that showed I was still in Ingolstadt: the magnificent tower of the Church of Our Lady, the old ducal castle, the Danube river flowing outside of the city's walls. These sites alone should have provided me enough evidence that the memories I possessed were real, but I still felt a great uneasiness concerning how much of my memories I could trust. These sites could have been embedded into the mind of any person who had ever been to Ingolstadt. As much as seeing these cherished landmarks raised my spirits, they did not prove that the rest of what seemed so real to me had not been imagined.

I crouched at the top point of the roof and searched the neighborhood until I spotted what I needed, which was on this very same street. The houses were situated so that they were close to one another, and in some cases their roofs were connected, and I was able to climb from one roof to another until I reached my destination. I then climbed down the building I was on and entered a tailor shop. Once inside I secured the door and closed the curtains so that no one from outside could look in. The tailor, a small and thin middle-aged man with even less hair covering his pink scalp than what the Marquis had had, sat hunched at a table as he worked on the construction of a coat. He shouted out his surprise on realizing that someone had entered his store and closed the window curtains without his permission, and demanded to know the reason for this, his voice high-pitched and quavering with indignation. Once he looked up at me his face fell slack, his eyes as fearful as if any other wild beast had wandered into his store.

"You will make for me a pair of trousers," I told him. "Also a hooded cape, with the hood large enough to hide my face."

He gulped noticeably, his eyes blinking rapidly as he stared at me. When he could talk, his voice came out in a squeak.

"Who will pay for this?" he asked.

I laughed at his question. How could I not? The sound of my laughter was something horrible and it caused the tailor to shudder and the blood to drain from his face.

"You may send the bill to Victor Frankenstein," I said.

"He has agreed to this?" the tailor asked.

I did not bother to answer him. A wretched look came over his face as he nodded. "I am busy now," he told me. "But if you come back next week I will have these articles ready for you."

I took a step closer to him in order to move further out from the shadows so that he could better see my face.

"You do not understand," I said. "Neither of us will be leaving your store until you have done as I asked."

"But look at your size!" he complained. "I am not sure I have the necessary materials in stock to make these items!"

"I am sure you will find a way even if it means tearing up articles of clothing that you have already made."

He nodded glumly, and after performing the odious task of measuring me, went to work. I watched for a few minutes, and then searched through a cabinet where I found a bottle of wine. My fingers were large and cumbersome but once I was able to grasp onto the cork I pulled it out easily without the need of a corkscrew. I drained the bottle in several gulps. The tailor watched this with amazement.

"I could find several more bottles of wine for you," he offered.

I stared at him indifferently, not bothering to answer him. Instead, I sniffed out a loaf of bread and cheese that had been stored away, and set upon to greedily consume my meager feast, leaving not even crumbs. The tailor repeated his offer to find me more bottles of wine. Of course I knew his purpose for this; that he hoped I would drink enough wine so that I would be dulled and fall unconscious. I glared at him and suggested he get back to work.

"Are you planning to murder me?" he asked.

"I have no intention of doing so," I said. "All I want is a pair of trousers and a hooded cape, and then you will not see me again."

He nodded and commenced his work, silently cutting and sewing material until he had a pair of trousers made for me. I put them on and found them satisfactory. He next proceeded to work on the cape, and was almost halfway done with it when he complained bitterly how he had been saving the bread and cheese that I had eaten as a later dinner for himself.

"So you will go to bed hungry tonight," I said. "That is not the worst hardship that can befall a man."

He frowned severely at this, but held back any arguments he might have had for me. While he worked at finishing the cape, I rummaged through his stock and found material that could be used for constructing coverings for my feet. While the skin covering my feet felt thick and tough, I did not know where my future travels were going to lead me, and felt it wise to be prepared in case I needed to visit harsher climates.

The tailor noticed the materials I held and asked about

them.

"You will be using these to fashion coverings for my feet."

He snorted indignantly at that. "I am not a cobbler," he stated.

"You are so close to completing my cape," I said. "Do not make these labors of yours for nothing."

He understood my implication. His face ashen, he hunched over the cape to add the hood so that he could be done with it. When he was finished, I slipped it on. A dressing mirror stood in the corner of the stop, and I crouched in front of it so I could see my reflection. The material used for the cape was black, which was better for hiding myself within, and the hood kept my face mostly hidden with only my knife-slit of a mouth showing. Even still, my reflection was of a hideous nature, and I knew I could not travel among men, not even with the concealment that the cape offered.

"Make those coverings for my feet so you can be done with me, and I with you," I said, my voice indicating a weariness that had come over me.

The tailor took offense at having to do the work of a cobbler and his nose wrinkled at the prospect, but he commenced with his work, and in little time fashioned for me the coverings that I desired. I slipped them on my feet and decided that they would make do.

"You have done what I have asked and I will keep my word," I told him, and I moved to leave his shop. As I removed the bolt that secured the door, he called out for me to stop. I turned and saw a look of consternation upon his face, as if he had a question of great importance that he wished to ask. I knew what it must be. To know what type of creature I was. Even though I had no idea how I could answer him, I told him to ask me his question.

"What is Herr Frankenstein's address?" he asked, boldly.

"I need it so I may send him the bill."

"When I find it I will let you know," I told him, and I left his store.

———∽∿∿∾———

I laid on a rooftop across from the Ingolstadt Apothecary. Dusk had started to descend, and shortly thereafter the lamps were extinguished within the apothecary. When Herr Klemmen exited the shop, a sadness welled up within my chest. The man who had been my employer for seven years and whose company I had greatly enjoyed used to be a robust figure with a cheerful countenance and a youthful appearance that belied his age. The man who exited the apothecary appeared to have aged a great many years. His posture was badly stooped and his hair, which had last seen only touches of gray, was now snow white. A tiredness seemed to have settled over his features, making him almost unrecognizable. But he had the same bushy tangle of eyebrows and thick mustache that I remembered, although they also had turned the same white as his hair. The changes in his appearance were so dramatic that they surprised me, and it made me wonder how much time could have elapsed between Friedrich Hoffmann's death and my birth within Frankenstein's laboratory. Could it have been as many years as his appearance seemed to indicate?

I knew the route that Herr Klemmen would take to arrive at his home, and I moved swiftly to an area that would be mostly in shadows so I could intercept him. I waited until he walked past my hiding spot before I called out to him.

He turned, alarm showing in his face. "Do I know you?" he asked.

I did not want my size or my appearance to frighten him, so I remained crouched in the shadows, the black cape that I wore mostly hiding me.

"Herr Klemmen," I said, "I come to you as a friend and

not to do you harm."

"Then show yourself to me."

"I cannot do so, for the hideousness of my appearance would distress you far more than the coarseness of my voice. I need to tell you that Friedrich Hoffmann never betrayed your trust. He was innocent of the murder of your beloved niece, Johanna."

Herr Klemmen put his hand to his heart, as if to keep it from breaking any further.

"That is impossible," he said, his voice pained. "My dear niece's locket was found in that villain's pocket, and his coat stained so with her blood. I demand that you tell me how he could be innocent!"

"The night before your niece's murder, a poison was slipped into an ale that Herr Hoffmann drank after his day's labor at your apothecary. This poison caused him to collapse into a state of unconsciousness in that same alley in which he was later found. While he lay helpless the true murderer stained his coat with blood and placed your dear niece's locket within Herr Hoffmann's trouser pocket, all so that he would be unfairly blamed for her murder."

Herr Klemmen's lips trembled as if he were on the verge of weeping. "How . . . how could you know this?" he asked.

"I will tell you, but first answer me this. In your heart do you believe Herr Hoffmann capable of this crime?"

Herr Klemmen's face appeared to crumble as he fought the tears that were struggling to come loose. He shook his head. "No," he said at last. "Friedrich was like a son to me. It is unimaginable to me that he could have acted in such a vile manner. Explain to me how you know of Friedrich's innocence?"

"I too have been greatly victimized by the same man whom I believe is responsible," I said, my voice sounding as a mere echo in my ears. "Once I have proven his guilt, I will avenge your niece's death. You have my promise."

"Has this villain disfigured you? Is this why you refuse to show yourself to me? You do not need to be afraid. Perhaps I have medicine within my store that could help you. Let us go back there together."

"I am beyond the help of medical science," I said. "Or anyone's help. Herr Klemmen, I do not wish to cause you any further sadness, and greatly regret the amount that my intrusion has caused, but I need to ask you a question that could further distress you."

"Do not regret anything, my son. Your words have the air of truth, and your visit has lifted a great weight from my heart, for now I can mourn Friedrich instead of despising him. What is it that you wish to know?"

"How long ago did this terrible crime occur?" I asked.

Herr Klemmen's jaw muscles tightened as he steeled himself to answer me. "We are two months short of the one year anniversary," he said.

Ten months! That was all it was? Herr Klemmen looked as if he had aged a decade, if not more, but it had only been ten months! I understood it. He never had children and had grown to think of his niece, Johanna, as his own child. I had also felt the warmth of fatherly love from him, so the circumstances must have been doubly tragic for him as Herr Klemmen had to suffer both grief and hatred together, and it took its toll. As I looked at Herr Klemmen's eyes brimming with tears, I felt the same tenderness and aching of love toward him as if he had been my true father, and I knew then that I had a soul. I don't know how that could have come to be, but I knew it was true, just as I knew that my memories of Johanna and my life as Friedrich Hoffmann were real, and not imaginary.

I hesitated before asking where Johanna was buried, Ingolstadt or Leipzig.

Gravely, his face aging even more, Herr Klemmen said, "My niece is now with her father and mother."

My voice barely came out as an animal growl as I said to Herr Klemmen, "You have my promise, sir. The man responsible for these terrible crimes will be made to suffer. Johanna Klemmen and Friedrich Hoffmann will be allowed to rest in peace."

I stole into the night then.

Chapter 8

I waited until dark before climbing over the twenty-foot wall that circled the city of Ingolstadt. The agility and strength within my new body was more that of a wild beast than a man, my limbs showing themselves to be sinewy and powerful, and I was easily able to leap so that I could pull myself over the wall and drop to the ground below. Once I was on the other side, I made my way down the banks of the Danube river and drank until I quenched the thirst that the earlier bottle of wine had merely tickled. Then I slipped into the woods, and using the stars to navigate, headed north toward Leipzig.

During my lifetime as Friedrich Hoffmann I had traveled to a few cities and villages outside of Ingolstadt, but never farther than Munich, and never outside of my homeland of Bavaria. Leipzig was over two hundred miles away, and in Saxony, which was unknown territory to me, but I had a burning need to visit my Johanna's grave. There was no longer any doubt that the memories I possessed as Friedrich Hoffmann were real, as was the compassion and love that I had felt for my betrothed, and the terrible grief that now weighed so heavily on me.

I thought about what Herr Klemmen had told me. That ten months had elapsed since Johanna's murder. From my own tally, I was held captive within Frankenstein's laboratory for almost seven months. Although it seemed as if it had only been seconds, three months had actually passed from my dying on the executioner's wheel to waking up in Frankenstein's company. For three months I had clearly been dead, and yet my soul and memories survived.

I had no idea where Frankenstein had run off to. No clues were left behind in his living quarters, and I could not recall him ever mentioning a destination that would be safe for him in the event he needed to flee. I did not know how I was going to find him, only that I would. Justice required it. But first I needed to travel to Leipzig so that I could leave flowers by Johanna's grave and say my prayers. Later, after I had paid the proper respects, providence would help me track down Frankenstein wherever he might be hiding.

As I made my way through the woods, I felt my senses keener than I could ever recall. I picked up smells in the woods that I never knew existed before, and I heard the distinctive cry of night owls far off in the distance, as well as small animals rustling in the underbrush. My vision changed the most dramatically. It was more that of a nocturnal beast than a man, and instead of stumbling in the dark I had little trouble making out my path. I should have been terrified with all the dangers that lurked around me, but instead I felt exhilarated. After all those months housed within the oppressive evil of Frankenstein's lair, the fresh air of the woods was a gentle balm to my spirits. For a time I even forgot about the hideousness of my present form, and imagined myself once more as I had been. But before too long those pleasant delusions vanished and my exhilaration proved short-lived.

I moved swiftly through the woods. Just as my agility and strength had grown greater than that of any man, so did my speed, and I ran more like the red deer that I had once hunted in my youth than I ever could have as Friedrich Hoffmann. After many hours of this I began to grow weary and for the first time since I had been brought back to life I desired sleep. I found a small cave to rest in, and after lying down I closed my eyes and silently said a short prayer.

Please, allow Johanna to visit me in my dreams. Even if it may only exist in the world of dreams, let my beloved bestow upon me one last sweet smile.

I dreamed, but it was not of Johanna. Instead my dreams were of a troubling and dark nature, as if I were being urged to turn away from Leipzig to instead head southwards. Before waking, an ominous gray castle appeared as if it were there to beckon me. The castle was of a ruined state and a foulness hung about it, the sight of it causing a cold chill to run through my heart. A great sense of relief overcame me when I woke and found myself back in the cave, and realized that that castle and the evil it represented were only phantoms.

I must have slept for only several hours, for it was not yet dawn when I awoke. The stars were gone, and without the sun rising to guide me, I had no method to determine which direction was north, but I chose to let my heart lead me to Johanna's grave. I had only traveled a short distance when I spotted the wolves. There were four of them facing me, all with their blue unmoving eyes staring intently at me, their gray and brownish fur matted, their backs hunched in a feral manner. They were silent as they began to move toward me, and as they broke into an all-out run, a primal fear swallowed me up and I turned to flee.

At first their snarls filled my consciousness and I felt their hot breath as they snapped at my ankles, but before too long I was outrunning them! That relief was short-lived as I realized I had been chased toward one of their waiting companions. This wolf was larger than the others. It stood crouched, its fangs glistening as it snarled. And then it was airborne as it sprung at me to rip out my throat. What happened next surprised me as much as it did this beast. I caught it in midair, one hand around the wolf's neck, the other gripping it by its hindquarters. Over a hundred pounds of beastly ferocity, and I held the animal suspended in midair, with the impact budging me only a step. The animal tried to little avail to squirm out of my grasp. I snapped its back as if it were little more than a dry tree branch and tossed its body onto the ground. For the first time I truly understood the strength that I possessed.

The other wolves had caught up to me and were circling me warily, with certainly some confusion as to why their time-honored hunting maneuver had failed to work. But they were hungry and even given my greater size, they mistook me for a man, which was a type of creature that they could normally overpower. I was no longer afraid. Instead I felt only regret that I was going to have to kill these beasts. As they circled me they edged closer, and two of them sprang at me at the same moment. I batted one of them away and caught the other by the scruff of its neck and threw it with enough force at one of the still circling wolves that I killed both of them. The last remaining wolf was not to be deterred. With all the beastly fury that it could muster, it charged at me and suffered the same cruel fate as its companions.

As I looked at their broken bodies lying on the ground, I felt only sympathy toward these animals. The wolf that I had batted away had landed against an oak tree and lay whimpering on the ground. A closer examination showed that its hindquarters were broken and that it had no chance for survival. Trying my best to soothe the animal during its last moments, I ended its suffering with a quick twist of its neck.

With a heavy heart I left the area and continued onwards, trusting my instincts to lead me north. An hour later when the sun began to rise, I was relieved to find that I was on the right path.

My journey to Leipzig took three days. Several times I

had to steal into villages to get my bearings, and once I surprised a gang of bandits, who, while blanching severely at
my appearance, provided me with the directions that I
sought. A few times I came across wayward and seemingly
dispirited troops from Napoleon's army, and while I considered doing my duty as a Bavarian citizen and sending them
into flight, images of the wolves that I left dead on the ground
invaded my thoughts, and instead I chose to avoid them.
They seemed miserable enough as it was without having a
daemon chasing them away.

During those three days I didn't feel the need to sleep
again, but did rest several times. I also found that a diet of the
mushrooms and berries that I came across in the woods was
sufficient.

Near the end of my journey I approached a woodsy area,
maybe three miles from Leipzig, and there I spotted a distin-
guished-looking man who appeared to be searching for different varieties of plants. He was a short man of slight build
and possessing a highly pronounced forehead, and dressed
finely in his white silk stockings, short tight trousers and dark
coat. I watched curiously as he examined different plants. I
grew suspicious, however, when he stopped at a nightshade
plant to collect its leaves. As I watched him my anger boiled
over.

"Another Voisin?" I yelled out.

My voice startled him and he nearly jumped out of his
buckled leather shoes. I stepped out from the trees that had
hidden me. His complexion paled as he saw me, but he did-
n't run away as others of late had done.

"Sir," he said, his voice showing none of his fright, his
eyes holding steady on me, "I am afraid you have me at a
disadvantage. But no, I am no Voisin. I assure you that I am
not a poisoner, notorious or otherwise."

Even with the hood hiding my face, I must have been a

frightful image with my enormous height and the ominous way in which I was clothed. Still, he stood his ground as I approached him.

"That is a nightshade plant whose leaves you are picking," I said. "I know for I was once a pharmaceutical chemist in the employ of the Ingolstadt Apothecary, as well as also having an interest in botany. The leaves are deadly and their only purpose is to poison. If you are not picking these leaves for mischief, then why are you?"

"I am collecting them for curative reasons and not harmful ones." His eyes all at once blazing with indignation, he added, "Sir, if you have been employed in the preparation of medicines, then you too have been up to your own share of mischief."

"Why would you say that?"

"Why? Because the accepted medical profession is barbaric!" He made a face to show his disdain, and had to take several deep breaths before he could continue. "I know of what I speak," he stated, his voice only slightly calmer. "I was trained as a doctor, and was employed as such for many years, and I can tell you that the tried and true methods employed today are absolutely primitive! Tell me, what is the point of bloodletting? To rob the patient of the vital fluids necessary for the restoration of health? And the harsh purgative medicines that doctors prescribe only to leave the patient in a weaker and more debilitating state? Bah!"

"I never performed any medical procedures," I said. "My profession required me to prepare the medications that were prescribed. Whether the purgatives that I would prepare were too harsh, I cannot say. But I do know that herbal balms that I produced for burns and rashes were effective."

"Yes, I know, and I did not mean to condemn you and your profession." He smiled at me benevolently, adding, "But I have seen firsthand the damage that doctors in their ignorance can cause, and it can be difficult for me at times to keep my temper in check. But I apologize for my outburst. Allow me to introduce myself. My name is Samuel Hahnemann."

That left me at a lost for several seconds before grunting out that my own name was Friedrich Hoffmann, which seemed a better choice than to introduce myself as a wretched abomination brought forth into the world by a wicked sorcerer. I shook my head at the hand that he held out to me. I was beginning to feel an affinity to this man, and I did not want him seeing the monstrous construction of my own hand. "My skin is sensitive to the touch," I said. "I cannot shake hands for that reason."

He peered at me curiously, but nodded. "You may believe that belladonna, or nightshade as you know it, can only be used as a poison," he said, "but taken in very low dosages I hope to prove that it can be curative. In fact, it may even be able to prevent scarlet fever."

"I have never heard of such thing."

"Nobody has," Herr Hahnemann said, smiling inwardly. "I have a belief of *like curing like*, and this is a theory that I have been experimenting with lately. The basic principle behind it is if a patient is showing symptoms similar to what the poisoning from a certain substance might cause, then that substance taken in minuscule portions will allow the body to heal itself. Just as belladonna poisoning will cause symptoms that are similar to scarlet fever, a small dosage of belladonna may very well act as a preventive treatment for that disease."

While Herr Hahnemann explained this to me, I could see him peering at me intently as if he were trying to discern what I might look like under my hood.

"You desire to see my face?" I asked.

"I apologize, Herr Hoffmann. You mentioned that your skin is sensitive to the touch, and I was wondering if that is why you are covering your head with a hood on such a mild day. Perhaps if you would accompany me back to my home, I could treat you using this new methodology that I am currently exploring."

"I do not wish to accompany you."

"Why? My home is only a short distance from here."

"It would be pointless. I am beyond the cure of any treatment."

"Nonsense! I do not believe that."

His face held only compassion. I shook my head. "Herr Hahnemann, I am a dead thing brought to life by dark satanic forces. There is no cure that could help me."

"Interesting," Herr Hahnemann said softly. "This is the reason you did not wish to shake hands earlier, and not because of your skin being sensitive?"

"Yes," I admitted. "My hands are of such a hideous nature that it would give you nightmares if you viewed them."

Herr Hahnemann stood rubbing his chin with one hand, his eyes appearing vacant as if he were deep in thought. When he looked back at me a light shone in those eyes.

"Herr Hoffmann, with the symptoms that you have expressed to me, I believe I can help you. If you accompany me to my home I will prepare a remedy for you."

"I cannot do that."

My answer frustrated him. Muttering softly to himself he began searching through the leather satchel that he carried. At last he found what he was looking for and held an envelope out to me.

"This envelope holds leaves from a jimson weed. I will explain to you how to produce a remedy from it. If you were once a pharmaceutical chemist, then you should be able to do this easily."

Jimson weed. *The Devil's trumpet. Hell's bells. The Devil's weed.* I couldn't help smiling as I thought of the other names that jimson weed was known as. I listened, though, as Herr

Hahnemann explained the procedure for producing a remedy from these leaves, which amounted to little more than generating a tincture, then mixing one drop of the tincture with eight ounces of water and a scruple of alcohol and mixing that vigorously. When he was done with his explanation he saw that I was not going to expose my hand to him by reaching for his envelope, and smiling gently, he placed the envelope instead by my feet. After that he nodded to me and went on his way. Once he was gone from sight, I picked up the envelope and fitted it within a pocket that the tailor had made within the inside lining of the cape. And then I continued on to Leipzig.

CHAPTER 9

When Johanna and I would talk of our future life together, my beloved had had only modest wants. She wished to have a home with a small garden where she could grow vegetables and herbs, and she wished to fill our home with many children, having been deprived of growing up within a large family, with her three older siblings dying unexpectedly before childbirth and her mother being unable to conceive again after her own birth. Johanna's face would light up so when she would tell me about the only true extravagance that she desired. To be able to travel back to her beloved city of her childhood so that she could share with me the many sights of Leipzig that had enchanted her in her youth. The botanical gardens that were the envy of all of Europe, the esplanade where she would stroll on Sundays with her father and mother, the St. Thomas Church where the great composer Johann Sebastian Bach had once been choir director, the city marketplace that she so loved and many other sights that had filled her with such fond and nostalgic memories.

I had waited until darkness fell before entering Leipzig so that I could roam the city unobserved and seek out Johanna's grave. It was as if an unseen hand guided me to the churchyard and her grave within it. While it was too dark for me to read her gravestone, I could feel the letters that had been engraved on the small slab of granite and knew that I had found Johanna. I sat on the ground next to where she was buried and felt a great emptiness well up within my chest as I thought of how futile it was that we were now in her childhood city together, and how even her most modest desires had been robbed from her.

That afternoon I had picked a bouquet of wildflowers for her. Bellflowers, daisies, wild roses and poppies, all of which she would delight in when I would surprise her with freshly picked bouquets back in Ingolstadt. As I placed these flowers by her gravestone, the gesture just seemed so insignificant. I tilted my head upwards toward the waxing crescent moon and howled out my agony, the sound emanating from me something horrible and unearthly. A great weariness overtook me and I collapsed to the ground.

My dearest Johanna, I am so sorry I was unable to protect you. You were the finest and most worthy person I had ever known, and nothing could be more monstrous than the crime that was committed against you. This will be avenged, and then I will join you. I promise you this.

A troubling thought occurred to me. What if I chased Frankenstein to the ends of the world only to find that he was innocent of Johanna's murder? It was possible that he was simply opportunistic in obtaining my brain for his foul experiment. Another villain for purposes unknown to me could have been behind these crimes, and Frankenstein's involvement could have been nothing more than to bribe the executioner for the material he sought. I could spend a lifetime chasing him only to see my promise to Johanna go unfulfilled.

But what else could I do than seek out Frankenstein?

The weariness that had descended on me left me too tired to think of vengeance. I closed my eyes and tried to think only of Johanna. It took a great effort but soon I pictured her the way she had looked on our last Sunday afternoon together. How contented she was as she rested her head against my shoulder while we sat together on the grassy knoll near the city hall. I could almost imagine the feel of her delicate hand as I had held it within my own. Tears streamed down my cheeks as I desperately clung to these memories. The weariness that I suffered had sunk heavily into my bones and weighed me down like stone. I could barely move and as my thoughts drifted away I fell into a sleep so deep that dreams could not invade it.

An animal instinct woke me. The sun had barely appeared in the horizon and a gray haziness filled the air. Moving stealthily toward me was a member of the clergy, and he carried a pitchfork as if his plans were to run me through. He was less than five feet from me, and as I was startled awake by his approach, he jumped backward, his large craggy face waxen in the faint early-morning light, his mouth opened to form a rigid circle.

"You are lying on hallowed grounds, daemon!" he swore at me, his eyes wide as they reflected a mix of fear and self-righteousness. "Do not blaspheme this area any further with your presence. Begone!"

"And what makes you so certain that I am a daemon?" I asked.

"Your hideousness marks you as such!"

My hood had fallen off my head during my sleep, exposing the full grotesqueness of my appearance. But I was not about to be chased away by this man.

"You do not know the goodness in my heart," I said. "Now leave me so that I may grieve alone."

He spotted the flowers then that I had placed by Johanna's grave, and his eyes took on a wicked look as his chest swelled with piety and a false bravery.

"One can only wonder at the evil nature of the witch that has been buried in this grave to attract a daemonic creature such as yourself. She will need to be dug up from these sacred grounds and her body burned. Now begone!"

He moved forward as if to stick me with his pitchfork. I grabbed it from him with the same quickness that I had displayed during my battle with the wolves. I rose to my full height so that I towered above him and only then did I snap the pitchfork in half and toss the pieces to the ground. The priest stood in front of me trembling, fear striking him so greatly that he couldn't speak or move.

"The child who rests here was of pure innocence and goodness," I said. I also trembled, but with me it was out of a burning rage. "If her grave is disturbed I will squash your head like a grape, and the vengeance that I will wreak on your church will be something horrible. Do you understand me?"

He was beyond speech, but his head nodded enough to show that he understood me. I turned from him before my rage led me to murder, and fled the churchyard. I kept running until I was out of the city and in the woods beyond.

Over the next seven days I kept vigil over Johanna. I found a great oak tree that I would climb each day, and with my keener vision, be able to watch for activity within the churchyard that Johanna was buried within. At night, under the cloak of darkness, I would visit her grave and rest by it. I was prepared to carry out my vengeance if her grave was disturbed, but the priest had heeded my words. After those seven days, I was satisfied that Johanna would be allowed to rest in peace, and I left the area of Leipzig and headed southwards toward my homeland of Bavaria.

While I kept vigil over Johanna I had many hours to sit in solitude and reflect on the violence and rage that now swirled through my heart, and these emotions frightened me. As Friedrich Hoffmann I had led a gentle life with barely any harsh thoughts pervading my mind, and certainly never any regarding revenge and murder. Now I was consumed with such thoughts, and it worried me that my soul might become as coarse as my outer appearance. What would vengeance ultimately bring me if these violent thoughts twisted my soul so that it would become unrecognizable to Johanna once I was finally allowed to quit this earth? But how could I ignore my promise to her? How could I allow such a terrible crime to go unpunished? These contradictory positions weighed heavily on me, and after many hours of pondering them   I decided that I would find Frankenstein and force him to admit the truth to me, and after that I would decide what I needed to do.

I wandered aimlessly for several days as the thoughts of how I would find Frankenstein tortured me. During these travels I avoided villages and cities, and headed instead into the darkest, most unknown regions of the forest, with my diet consisting solely of berries and mushrooms and nuts that I was able to forage. While I rested several times, I did not sleep. My mind was too troubled with thoughts for sleep to have been possible.

One morning I broke through a dense thicket of thornbushes and small trees to find myself at the base of a valley. As I peered down into it, I saw acres of vineyards growing. I had been under a heavy shelter of elm trees and black locust and mountain ash that had made the forest seem like night, but now as I stood in a clearing I could see the sun was already present in the sky, its rays warm upon my face, and the pleasantness of the scene filled me with a serenity that seemed so foreign to me. I made my way further into the valley to inspect these vines. When I reached them I sampled several bunches of grapes and tasted their sweetness and stood puzzling over this mysterious vineyard. It was then that I spotted to my right a great stone structure that appeared to be a monastery. This made as little sense to me as these vineyards. I knew I had traveled deep into the forest, far from any village or city, so why would a monastery be out here? I moved back to the edge of the woods so that I could investigate this mysterious monastery without being seen.

As I crept through the woods toward this structure, a group of monks appeared as they ambled toward the vineyards to pick grapes. I found a spot where I could watch without their knowledge. I had been without the company of man for many months, for I could not consider Victor Frankenstein or his guest, the Marquis, members of the race, and I took comfort in watching their simple labors. Even though I was apart and hidden from them I felt their camaraderie. I was still puzzled over the existence of this hidden monastery, but I took joy in watching these men pick their grapes. All of them were dressed in the same modest manner: brown robes with a rope tied around their middle and with leather sandals protecting their feet. There was a simplicity in their lives that I longed for. I was so involved in watching them that I had failed to notice that one of their members from the monastery had discovered me, for he was now standing next to me. I didn't realize this until he had placed a hand lightly on my shoulder.

"You seem to be enjoying our brothers' labors," he said.

He was dressed in the same style of brown robe and sandals as the monks who worked the vineyards. A short, round man with a circle of graying hair surrounding his pink scalp. His eyes shone only with benevolence as he smiled at me. I understood why my instincts had failed to alert me of his approach. There was nothing to fear from this man.

I turned my look away from him and back toward the monks and their labor.

"Ever since I was old enough to be employed, I have worked diligently," I said. "My current idleness does not suit me. So, sadly, I must find my comfort in watching others enjoy their labor."

"And how were you employed?"

"As a chemist."

"Why are you no longer employed as such?"

"Because I am no longer fit for the company of man," I said, my voice dropping to a low and awful whisper. "Can you not tell from the ungodly nature of my voice? My appearance is likewise hideous."

To prove this I removed the hood from my head.

"My son, did this happen from a terrible accident? A fire?"

I turned back to look at him, and was surprised to see that his expression only reflected concern. Not even a hint of fear or disgust could be seen.

I nodded. My voice was only a soft rumble as I told him, "At one time I was as fair as any other man, but I suffered a cruel fate. When I awoke, this is how I looked."

"And this is why you have wandered off into the middle of the forest? To hide from man?"

"For the time being," I admitted. "I was surprised to find a monastery in such a hidden part of the forest. It seems like an odd place for it to have been built."

"This is the perfect location for us to have built it," he said. "We are far from the intrusion of governments and warring armies. France's invading forces won't stumble upon us here, nor our own Prussian armies. Here we are free from the troubles of the world to make our wine and live our lives in quiet contemplation, and a hidden road allows us to sell our wine without fear of discovery. My name is Brother Theodore. How may I address you?"

"My name was once Friedrich Hoffmann," I said. "Of what monastic order are you?"

Brother Theodore chuckled at that, his round body bouncing under his robe. "Of one that you have never heard, Brother Friedrich, I assure you." His smile turned more solemn as he continued to gaze at me. "Here we do not judge men by their appearance but by what is in their heart, and we will grant any lost traveler sanctuary. We offer a simple life here; the quiet companionship of your fellow man and an honest day's labor. What do you say, Brother Friedrich, would you like to quit this idleness that you earlier expressed unhappiness with to once again seek the fulfillment that honest labor can provide?"

"I have a mission that I must carry out," I said.

"Surely this mission does not have to be carried out today? We can offer sanctuary for a day, a month or a lifetime, whatever your soul requires, and Brother Friedrich, I sense a great uneasiness within you, and I believe you could benefit from rejoining the company of your fellow man, even if it is only for a day."

My gaze was fixed on the monks toiling in the field below, and I felt overwhelmed with the desire to join them. "I do not know," I said.

"Let me sit with you for a spell while you consider it," Brother Theodore said, and he sat on the ground nearby me, his gaze also fixed on the monks working the vineyards below us. After a half hour in this quiet solitude, I asked Brother Theodore how the other monks would react to the hideousness of my appearance.

"The same as me," Brother Theodore said. "They would recognize a troubled but gentle heart, and they would welcome you without hesitation."

I sat with a heavy heart as I contemplated Brother Theodore's offer while at the same time being pulled to keep my promise to Johanna. Then, almost as if Johanna were whispering in my ear, I had this sense of her telling me that for now I should accept the solace that Brother Theodore was offering.

With tears flooding my eyes, I told Brother Theodore my decision.

CHAPTER 10

They had no brown robes large enough to fit me, so it was decided that for the time being that I could continue to wear my cape. The cell I was assigned held a cot and a window, and nothing else. The cot was too small for me, and Brother Theodore agreed to let me fashion some bedding out of straw and blankets. Even so, the space making up my cell was too small to allow me to lie down unless I did so on my side with my knees pulled to my chest.

Instead of working the vineyards, it was agreed that my great strength could be better utilized in pressing the grapes, and I was soon performing the labor of twenty men. My first evening when I sat with the other monks around the large dining table that held over sixty men, the other monks showed me the same compassion that Brother Theodore had. At Brother Theodore's urging I had left my face uncovered by the cape's hood, and none of the other monks displayed any distress over my appearance, nor did any of them appear to notice the monstrous construction of my hands. Instead they only favored me with warm smiles and gentle nods and the good cheer of camaraderie.

Dinner was a simple meal of bread, cheese, greens and wine, but it was difficult to remember a meal that I had enjoyed more. After the meal's completion we all returned to our cells for quiet meditation and sleep. At no time were words spoken, or were they necessary.

I didn't sleep that night, but I enjoyed the solitude, and the next morning as the sun broke into the sky, I left my quarters refreshed and ready for a day of productive labor.

Words were rarely spoken within the monastery, with the monks preferring to communicate through simple gestures and warm smiles. After the completion of my second week, Brother Theodore approached me as I cleaned the vats. I was surprised to hear his voice as he told me that due to my efforts the monastery had produced a record amount of wine.

"You are spoiling us, Brother Friedrich," he continued. "Because of your labors we are finding ourselves able to spend more of our time in quiet contemplation. You have been a godsend to us, and I hope that being amongst us has been equally good to you."

"It has, Brother Theodore," I admitted. "More and more I am feeling the same contentment that I did in my former life."

This was mostly true. Not only did the brothers make me feel welcome, but they also treated me as if I were an equal member of their brotherhood, and at times I would even forget about my hideous appearance. But I didn't tell Brother Theodore about the pull on my soul that I felt nightly to seek out my enemy, Victor Frankenstein, nor the troubling nature of my dreams when I would sleep. They were always the same, always filled with a dark foreboding. As with the pull that I would feel on my soul, these dreams were also urging me to leave the monastery and head southwards. Always that ruined castle would be lurking in the background beckoning me, and at times I would even hear Frankenstein's voice taunting me. Whenever I would wake from these dreams it would take a great effort on my part to stay within my cell and not flee the monastery for the dark woods beyond. More and more I tried not to sleep at night, but with my daily labors I was finding sleep harder to ignore, and would drift off every third night or so for several hours only to wake in a disturbed state.

That night I had slept, and Brother Theodore sensed the uneasiness within me, for a sadness showed in his eyes as he favored me with a smile.

"There is still much troubling your heart, Brother Friedrich," he said.

"Less each day, Brother Theodore," I told him, which was again mostly true. The unease from the night before would usually leave me once I had rejoined the company of the other brothers and been fully engaged for several hours with my daily labor. For the rest of the day I would barely feel the pull on me to leave.

"That is good," Brother Theodore said. "As you know we try to refrain from speaking, although none of us have taken a vow of silence. It is only that freedom from the spoken word provides us a solitude that we prefer. There are times, though, when words are necessary, especially for many of our new members who arrive here with heavy hearts. If you ever feel the need to unburden yourself with speech, please know that I am always available."

I nodded my gratitude to him. Each night, though, the pull on me to leave the monastery grew stronger. It didn't matter whether I slept or lay awake on my bedding, during those dark bewitching hours the urge pulling me away would become something both terrible and irresistible. This growing compulsion was as if something were pounding in my head, like the beating of savage drums. I could barely stand it, and by the first rays of the morning light I would be drenched in sweat as every muscle in my body strained to keep me from fleeing my cell. After four months I found that this urge continued long into the day, with not even my hard labors sufficient to beat it down. After the completion of another week's stay within the monastery, I told Brother Theodore that I had to leave.

"Brother Friedrich, we are in the dead of winter. Would not it be better to wait until spring? I fear you entering into the wilderness in this harsh weather."

"No. I cannot wait."

He nodded as he accepted what I said. "You will be sorely missed, Brother Friedrich," he said, his eyes brimming with a genuine sadness. "And not because of your great labors, but because of the warmth and compassion that you have bestowed upon us. I do fear that you will find the world that you will be entering every bit as harsh as these winter winds, as they rarely look beyond a man's physical appearance to what resides in his heart. I worry about how you will be treated, but I know I cannot persuade you to stay against your wishes. Could you tell me what it is that has been troubling you so greatly, for I know it is far more than the accident that disfigured you. Perhaps by unburdening yourself your desire to leave us will lessen?"

I relented then and told Brother Theodore what had happened to my dearest Johanna. Up until that moment I had blocked out from my consciousness the terrible things that were said during my trial about the despicable acts that were committed against Johanna, but as I told Brother Theodore how her body had been so horribly violated before her murder a great anguish filled me and I became afraid that I would start tearing down walls with my very hands if I didn't leave.

Brother Theodore's face reflected his alarm. "My son, the tale you have told me is indeed awful, and one can only imagine your thirst for vengeance. But this will only lead you to ruin. Salvation will come from forgiveness. I implore you, do not let this wicked villain darken your soul any further. Even if you must leave here, find a way to banish this thirst for vengeance that is so consuming you."

I shook my head, my body trembling with violence. Without another word I raced from the dining room where we were speaking and out of the monastery doors and to the woods beyond its walls, afraid of the terrible crimes I would wreak on these innocent monks if I stayed another minute.

CHAPTER 11

My obsession to seek out Victor Frankenstein only intensified after I left my brother monks, and at times I thought I would go mad hearing Frankenstein's voice whispering to me as if his lips were only inches from my ear, both daring me and commanding me to find him. Over the next several months an insanity took me over. At nighttime I would steal into whatever nearby city or village I had arrived at the outskirts of during the day, and I would search for my enemy, often spying into windows and skulking through darkened homes. Some nights I would be discovered, and the innocent man or woman doing so would scream out in fear or swoon straightaway at the sight of me, but that didn't deter me, and neither did the loathing that consumed me. As much as I despised myself for these noxious activities I was engaged in, I felt as if I had little control over my actions; as if I were little more than a puppet and invisible strings were controlling my movements.

The cold chill of the winter air had little effect on me; neither did the snow or freezing rain. I would spend my days either hiding in nearby woods or traveling to the next city or village. Sometimes I would spot men armed with muskets and swords searching the woods for me, but they were easy to elude, and the hounds that they would send after me had no better luck picking up my trail. In my growing madness, I would sometimes amuse myself by climbing the tallest oaks to watch them searching fruitlessly for me. Once darkness arrived, I would sneak among these people like a fiend to perform my own search, for Victor Frankenstein.

It was sometime during the last vestiges of winter, when the days were growing longer and the weather more pleasant, and the dirt roads had been transformed into little more than rutted mud, when I found myself back in my native Bavaria. That day I had traveled to the outskirts of a small village that was not more than a half day's journey from Ingolstadt, and I hid in the woods close enough to where I could see several cottages. When night arrived, I once again engaged in seeking out my enemy, sneaking through one home after another. As I was searching though a stone cottage on the other side of the village, a young girl surprised me. She could have been no older than twelve, and was the picture of innocence as she stood in front of me in her long nightgown, her face freckled, her long yellow hair falling like fine spun silk past her frail shoulders. I could see so much of my dear Johanna in her innocence and her budding beauty, and when she asked me if I was there to murder her and her family and eat their bodies, it was as if a fever broke and the dreadful fog that had been enveloping my mind lifted.

"I am not here to do you or your family harm," I said.

"Then why are you here?" she asked.

I did not know how to answer her. How could I explain the madness that drove me to such a fruitless activity? How could I possibly have expected to find Frankenstein with this haphazard searching of dwellings that I had been engaged in? Even if I had searched every home in Bavaria, what could I have hoped to accomplish? As I looked into the fear that shone in her eyes and accepted my culpability in its creation, and worse, saw how I was becoming the same abomination on the inside that I was outwardly, I fell to my knees and began to weep. My weeping continued until this same child later touched me lightly on the shoulder. When I looked up she offered me a piece of chocolate.

"You must have come into our home because you are

hungry and needed food," she said. "Here, please take this chocolate. I would give you more but this is all that I have saved from my birthday from last week."

I took the chocolate from her. What else could I have done while she looked at me with such earnest charity? With the chocolate crumbling in my hand, I left the cottage and soon quit the village as I continued on into the woods.

I walked for many miles until taking a seat on a fallen tree that must have succumbed to the forces of nature many years earlier, and leaned forward so that my elbows rested on my knees, and dropped my head so that it lay heavy in my hands. I longed to be back within the gentle confines of the monastery, but even if I could find my way back to that hidden sanctuary, how could I face Brother Theodore after what I had done since leaving? And what would he now see in my heart?

When I had first woken up within Frankenstein's lair, I had felt as if I were still Friedrich Hoffmann. Later, when I was employed and living freely among my fellow brothers at the monastery, I would also frequently envision myself as how I used to be and not as the abomination that I had become. My thirst for vengeance had brought about a madness that left me terrorizing the countryside for months, and now I could only think of myself as something ugly and twisted. My chest ached every time I imagined that young girl's face and the sheer terror that had filled her eyes.

Even if I could retrace my steps, I could not go back to that monastery. Not with the way Brother Theodore and the other monks would look at me, and not with that urge that was still pulling me southwards. Although I now seemed free from that the invisible force that had made me perform my sinister nighttime excursions as surely as if I had been possessed by spirits and then exorcised, that same urge from before was still present within me. And the truth was that even if that madness had left me, I still thirsted for vengeance.

I sat for hours as I tried to make sense of everything that had happened since I had first woken up within Frankenstein's laboratory. If that young girl had reported my unwelcome intrusion into her home, I didn't see any evidence of it since no armed mobs had come searching for me. Given the muddy conditions, if a mob was looking for me they would have had no trouble following my footprints since I made no effort to hide them. But if a mob had come I would have offered no resistance. Death would have been a welcome release from the self-loathing and confusion that consumed me.

When dawn arrived, I left the fallen tree that I had been seated on so despondently and continued my aimless wandering.

———

Over the next six days I avoided man as best I could and tried to keep my wanderings to the darker depths of the forest. Early on I came across a lost troop of French soldiers who seemed every bit as miserable as I was. I stayed hidden under a canopy of leaves and branches and watched them as they argued about a number of subjects, including their whereabouts and their dwindling supplies. A couple of them insisted vehemently that they never would have embarked on this campaign if they had known that a devil had been let loose within the Bavarian countryside. When I saw what must have been their commanding officer trying to silence their squabbling with the threat of his saber, I had seen enough and stole quietly away. I shuddered minutes later when I heard the eruption of fighting among them and the death cries that followed. They were as damned as I was.

As I continued with my travels I would go back and forth in my mind between despairing over whether I would ever find Victor Frankenstein to desiring to quit Europe and flee

instead to the darkest jungles of the Amazon so I would for-
ever be free of man and my damnable quest for vengeance.
All of this left me weary, but I did not allow myself to sleep.
I was too afraid of the dreams that would invade my mind.

It was on the sixth day after the feverish control over
me had broken that I found myself wandering aimlessly
through the forest and my thoughts interrupted by the
shouting of men. They seemed to be arguing heatedly, with
several of them claiming that the Devil had been unleashed
upon their countryside and that that by itself proved the existence of witches. This got me curious, and I followed their
voices to see what this was about. Keeping myself hidden
behind a thick covering of bushes, I saw that I had wandered near a village. A group of forty or so men and women
stood in front of a small wooden cottage, their faces reflecting anger and excitement. As I followed their argument,
it seemed as if most of them were in agreement that the
woman living in the cottage was a witch, with one lone man
trying to argue the ridiculousness of their charges. This man
was middle-aged and of strong bearing. Tall, broad shouldered, thick-jawed. He was patiently trying to explain how
the belief in witchcraft had rightfully been banished from
the minds of all but the most ignorant. One of his oppo-
nents, a round-bodied man who had the look of a butcher,
took exception to this.

"You calling us ignorant then, Karl?" this man demanded.

"No, I'm not saying that. But let us not travel back a
hundred years to those dark years when superstitions ruled.
We live in an enlightened age. We now know witches never
truly existed. This has been proven beyond any doubt. How
could they exist under the watchful eye of the Almighty?"

"Then how do you explain the appearance of Satan? If
Satan is running free in the countryside, then there are certainly witches to do his bidding!"

"Come now, Ernst. Let us not jump to conclusions. We do not know that anything has been seen. All we are hearing are fanciful stories, that is all."

"Fanciful stories? So you are calling them all liars?"

"I am saying that the same hysteria that caused people seventy years ago to burn and drown innocent men and women as witches may be making people now believe they are seeing a devil when all they could be seeing is a wild beast, perhaps an exceptionally large bear, and imagining in their hysteria that this animal is something supernatural."

"And what of the girls who are being stolen?"

"Again, these are just stories! If you really believe this nonsense about Henriette being a witch, then let us bring her to a court and have them decide her guilt."

A woman's voice shrilly interrupted them, yelling out that there was no question about this witch's guilt. The voice belonged to a plain woman of around thirty who had pushed herself to the front and stood red-faced in front of Karl, the man who was trying to reason with them.

"She has bewitched my husband!" this dumpy frau insisted. "We can prove right now that this is so, unless you are in league with her and wish to keep her evil hidden from us!"

This last accusation of hers got the heavyset butcher scowling suspiciously at Karl, as well as several of the other men edging closer to him. He noticed this and realized that he himself was close to being accused of being a witch, and a cautiousness set into his eyes as he closed his mouth and did not argue any further.

A young woman was dragged to the front by several men. She was of a different type from the frau. Although her dress was little more than rags, it did little to hide the suppleness of her body. Even in her dire situation and with the contempt toward her accusers that hardened her expression, her heart-shaped face and fire-red hair radiated beauty.

Her right hand was grabbed, and the butcher cut it with a knife to draw blood. This blood was then marked on the forehead of a small, timid-looking man who stood next to the frau, and who must have been her husband. Once the blood was spread over his forehead, he yelled out that he was no longer bewitched.

"This witch's spell has been broken," he exclaimed. He turned to look at the frau and with a forced smile added, "I no longer desire her, but once again only desire my dear wife!"

"There never was any spell!" the red-haired young woman insisted. "Herr Brunnow is a lecher who has many times tried to put his hands on me! The only reason he has had little desire for his wife is because she is shaped similarly to a hog!"

The wife in question stepped forward to slap this young woman but instead fell to the ground in convulsions. That seemed to be the final straw and the young woman was dragged away while others went to the aid of the convulsing victim. Karl, the man of reason who had tried earlier to argue sense to this mob, stood by helplessly and watched.

I could barely believe what I was seeing. Marking a victim of a bewitching with the witch's blood to break a spell was an old wives' tale that had long ago been forgotten, and here it was being dragged out again. Was I the cause of this? Was my being seen in other cities and villages the cause of this resurgent belief in witches? I watched, dumbfounded, as the wood cottage the young woman was thrown into was set ablaze.

They were going to burn her alive.

Without any thought of the consequences I rushed out from my hiding place. At first there was little more than looks of dumbfounded amazement on the faces of the members of the mob in front of me, then several of the men tried to block my advance, but once I knocked them aside, the others ran off. I kicked in the door of the burning cottage and dashed in without breaking stride. The young woman inside lay collapsed on the floor. The fire had yet to consume her, but the smoke was thick inside, and it must have been suffocating her. Although my eyes began to tear badly and the flames licked at my body, I made my way through so I could carry her out to safety. I held her in my arms as I ran from the burning cottage. Once outside, my path was blocked. Many of the men had armed themselves with pitchforks and other weapons and stood waiting for me. The frau still lay flopping around on the ground as if some unseen force had a grip on her and was shaking her like a child would a rattle. Her husband ignored this to point a bony finger at me and shout that I was proof that the woman was a witch. That the Devil himself had come to rescue her.

I slung the young woman over my shoulder, and as the men came toward me with their weapons I batted them aside—not hard enough to kill them but hard enough to send them flying. Soon a path opened up before me and I ran, ignoring the shouts and curses of the men behind me. Within seconds I entered the forest and the safety that it offered. I kept running until I had left the village far behind me. When I came to a clearing and a soft bed of grass, I lay the young woman upon it.

She was unconscious and her breathing remained shallow. While my field of study was chemistry, I had a small understanding of medical procedures, and understood that her breathing was being restricted by the smoke that she had inhaled. I needed to breathe fresh life into her or she might. perish where she lay. Gingerly I opened her mouth and blew air into her. After a minute of this she began coughing, and I backed away from her. When she opened her eyes and they focused on me, a dismal look weighed on her features.

"Am I in Hell?" she asked, her voice weak, the effects of the smoke still heavy on her. "Is that why Satan is standing over me?"

"I am not Satan," I said. "I am a passerby who rescued you from the mob who tried to burn you within your cottage. You are still alive and of this earth."

She closed her eyes, and for a long moment I became worried that the fire had ended her life regardless of my efforts. But I detected that she was still breathing, even if only shallowly, and her eyes opened again. This time they held a dullness to them as she stared at me.

"You have taken me to feast on my flesh," she said in a despondent whisper.

"Why would you say that?"

"That is what is being said. That a daemonic fiend has been stealing young girls to feast on them."

I shook my head. "My diet is mostly what I forage in the forest. Berries and mushrooms. I took you from that burning cottage to rescue you, and for no other purpose."

She thought about that for several minutes, a look of deep consternation ruining her brow.

At last, she said, "If that is true then I must be a witch after all. I did not believe it when that hag Frau Brunnow accused me, but why else would a daemonic creature suddenly come to my rescue?"

"You are not a witch, since they do not exist, and I am not a daemonic creature," I said, although I was not at all sure of that anymore. Dark, satanic magic breathed life into the hideous form that I now resided within, and if it wasn't the Devil behind the feverish obsession that had sent me skulking through homes in my search for Victor Frankenstein, then what could it have been? Still, though, I prayed that my soul hadn't been completely eroded, and that some of Friedrich

Hoffmann's sensibilities still resided within my heart.

Her eyes grew puzzled at she looked at me. "Then what are you?" she asked.

"I was once a man," I said. "Terrible things were done to me, but I believe I still hold some of my former goodness."

She did not look convinced, but she was too weak to do much more than close her eyes. I used my cape to clean her face, which had been darkened with soot, and then I went to off to find her water and food. During my earlier nighttime excursions, I had stolen a flask. When I found a spring flowing with fresh water I filled this flask that I now carried on me, and after finding a raspberry bush, I returned back to her. She accepted the water and berries that I offered her, and after several minutes she regained the strength to sit up.

"What will become of me?" she asked.

"You will rest until you are able to travel, and then I will take you to a new village where you will be safe."

Her face darkened as she considered this. "There is no such village," she said. "Whether or not you are a daemonic creature, it does not matter. Word will spread throughout the countryside of how the Devil rescued me from being burned alive as a witch. Anywhere I go they will now believe that I am a witch, and they will burn me also."

This was true. Stories of this kind spread quickly.

"Then I will take you to a foreign land where nobody has heard of this. I will see you safe before I leave you."

She gave me a hopeless look to show that she did not believe that that would be possible, but she was too tired and weak to argue, and instead closed her eyes and drifted into a sound sleep.

I watched her for a moment, and then after laying my cape over her, I gathered firewood so that she would be warm enough when night fell.

CHAPTER 12

When morning came and she opened her eyes and saw me standing guard over her, she looked up at me with an expression devoid of any emotion and without a single reflection of the hideousness of my appearance, which, without my cape to conceal me, was fully exposed to her. "It was not a nightmarish dream as I had hoped it was," she said.

"I am afraid not."

She deliberated on this, a hardness settling over her features as she did so. When she was done, the hardness faded leaving behind vulnerability. "I suppose if you had ill intentions toward me you would have acted on them already. It is true that you only wished to save my life?"

"Yes."

"Thank you then," she said. "And thank you also for covering me with your cape to keep me warm. But you may reclaim it. I can already feel the sun's rays upon my face."

"Later," I said. "There is still a chill in the air."

She nodded and closed her eyes again. "I am afraid I am too weak to stand."

"That is to be expected. You will rest here until your strength has returned, and then I will take you someplace where you will be safe and can start life anew. Someplace where stories of your rescue will not haunt you. Perhaps Geneva?"

"Perhaps." A bare wisp of a smile showed on her lips. "I do not know what to call you."

"Friedrich."

Her eyes opened a crack as she acknowledged me. "And you may call me Henriette."

And then her eyes were closed again and she was back asleep.

———ﾟﾟﾟ———

I cared for Henriette over the three days that it took for her to regain her strength. During this time I fetched her water and food as needed, watched over her to keep the wild beasts of the forest away, kept the fire burning to keep her warm, made a balm from herbs to apply to her cut hand, and over her protestations I covered her each night with my cape. The times that she lay awake we would talk. She told me how she had lived her whole life in the village of Aibling, and how she had been orphaned as a young child and had been put to work at the age of twelve in the village's beer hall.

"It hasn't been bad," she said as she explained the simple life that she had led. "At the beer hall they would have me clean the glasses and bring beer to the customers. That was fine. It was only when lechers like Herr Brunnow believed that the cost of an ale entitled them to also pinch my bottom that I detested my work." She giggled, adding, "Two weeks ago, Herr Brunnow tried to grab me outside of the beer hall and I kneed him in a sensitive area. That is why he has been unable to show any enthusiasm toward the sow that he married."

All at once she began to weep.

"What is wrong?"

She shook her head, her eyes showing her fury. "How could they accuse me of being a witch?" she demanded. "I have lived with these people my whole life. How could they do that to me? Because of Frau Brunnow's jealous accusations? Because I dared to rebuff other men's advances? And how will I live somewhere else?"

"You will. There is much strength in you. I can tell that. Soon, as you are starting a new life in Geneva, this will all be but a bad dream."

Henriette used her palms to wipe the tears from her eyes, and this left her pale skin blotchy and her eyes reddish. "I do not think Geneva would be safe for me," she said. "We have had travelers from Geneva pass through Aibling. They speak the same language as us. Stories of my being rescued by the Devil could end up there."

I had to agree. Geneva was too close, and there was too much commerce between Bavaria and the Swiss Confederation, and many of the Swiss were fluent in both German and French.

"I will take you to Italy then. Perhaps Venice?"

She showed me a fragile smile. "I cannot speak the language."

"I can teach you Italian."

She opened her eyes wide at that, and I explained how I was well versed in many languages other than my own native German, including Italian, French, English and the ancient languages of Latin and Greek. "At a very young age I was a student of languages," I told her. "Once I decided on a course of study in chemistry at the University, I studied languages even more intently so that I would not have to wait for translations to be able to read papers on subjects of interest. In fact, I supported myself while engaged at the University by translating other works into German."

I proceeded to rattle off phrases in different languages, and that impressed her, and when I felt a smile wrinkle my own face, she smiled back at me with a pleasantness that warmed my heart. We agreed then that I would teach her Italian during our travel to Venice. This meant we would have to cross the Alps, and I was not sure how I would be able to do that with Henriette, but decided that I would somehow find a way. I kept my worry to myself. The poor girl had enough as it was to worry about.

Once Henriette regained enough strength to walk, we

headed northeast, toward Munich. Travel with her was slow, and I wished I could have left her to rest more, but I did not trust leaving her alone with the wolves and bears and other wild beasts that lurked in the forest, and I needed to reach a city so that I could continue my thieving ways. This time, though, I felt justified in what I was going to be stealing, for these were articles needed if Henriette was going to survive the trip to Venice, as well as her being able to live a good life there. I was better read than Henriette and knew what to expect. In Geneva, they treat their servants as family, and she could have been happy there, except that she was right—the stories from Aibling could follow her to Geneva. In Venice, if the stories I read were true, a young and beautiful girl like Henriette without any money or family to protect her could very well be forced to become a whore to survive, and I was not about to let that happen. I felt responsible for her current situation. If it was not for my earlier skulking and the wild stories that spread because of it, Frau Brunnow would not have been able to get very far accusing Henriette of being a witch, and Henriette would now be safe and still happy in Aibling.

When we were several miles away from Munich, I built a fire for Henriette to sit by, hoping that that would be sufficient to keep her safe, and once darkness came I raced toward the city.

This time I did not have a fever blinding me and I was more careful in my thieving and skulking, and my activities went unnoticed. I picked only the largest and wealthiest homes to rob, and I ended up with an attire for Henriette that was better suited for the travel we were going to be undertaking, as well a sack full of gold and precious gems that would assure Henriette of a good life in Venice. I also took several bundles of food that were better suited for her than what I had been foraging, as well as several bottles of wine. Once I had all of this, I raced back to where I had left Henriette. The fire was still burning, and she was safe. I was crouching as I showed her what I had brought for her, and she squealed with delight and threw her arms around my neck and kissed my cheek.

Embarrassed, I waited until she let go of my neck before I wiped the wetness of her kiss from my cheek. "I do not know if there are beer halls in Venice," I explained. "And I do not wish for you to have to pour wine instead."

"Thank you, Friedrich, for all of your kindness." Concern ruined her smile as she stopped to consider what I had done. "About the people that you stole from?"

"They were wealthy. They can afford charity to an unfortunate young woman who was unfairly accused of a ridiculous crime and was almost burned to death because of it. Do not worry about them. Let us sleep now, for we have many miles to travel tomorrow."

Henriette agreed, and she lay on a soft bed of grass next to where I had built a fire. Once she was asleep, I covered her with my cape to provide her additional warmth. As usual since she had been in my care, I did not sleep, and instead stood guard over her. I was grateful for this diversion, for it allowed me to keep my own awful dreams at bay.

CHAPTER 13

To help Henriette learn Italian more thoroughly, I decided that we would converse only in that language, but she had an agile mind and was a quick learner, and within five days of our travel toward the Swiss Alps, she showed a mastery of the language that surprised me. There were times when she would be frustrated as she would try to remember words or figure out how to phrase her statement, and this frustration would show in the way her eyes would squint and her lips would compress, but in the end she would work out how to say what she wanted. Usually it would be questions about my life in Ingolstadt, and I would answer her freely, although I never would talk about Johanna. When she asked what type of accident or fire had made me look the way I did, and how I came to be of such gigantic size, I told her that I did not know—that all I remembered was suffering great injuries and what happened afterward to transform me was a mystery to me. I did not wish to tell her about Victor Frankenstein or about the unholy manner in which I was constructed.

Travel with Henriette was slow, as I would often have to clear away bramble and other obstacles for her, but I greatly enjoyed her companionship and quickly developed a deep affection for her. This affection was not of the type that I had felt toward Johanna, but more as if Henriette were a dear cousin or sister.

It was after a week of our travel together that we escaped the darkest part of the forest to lighter woods with glens and finally just a scattering of trees. This allowed us to make greater progress, although Henriette's pace was still considerably slower than what I could have made on my own. As we walked more freely, Henriette was in a particularly cheerful mood, her eyes sparkling as she joked of how instead of my taking her to Venice, we should instead build a cabin in the woods and live together.

"Not as husband and wife," she said, "but as brother and sister, for that is how I have grown to think of you, Friedrich."

"A fine life that would be for you," I said, but I had grown distracted for off in the distance were wolves. Five of them. They were keeping their distance, but they were tracking us, nonetheless. Henriette spotted them also, and edged closer to me so that our bodies touched.

"Why do you suppose they are following us like that but not moving closer?" she asked, her voice tight with fear. "It is almost as if they are wary of us."

I wondered this also. Could these wolves somehow know how I had slaughtered their brethren when they had attacked me, and was this the reason for their cautiousness? As we walked, the wolves maintained their distance, but they also continued to track us, and I could sense Henriette's growing nervousness over this. I picked up a stone and threw it with all my strength at them, hitting one of the wolves in its hindquarters. The wolf let out a surprised yelp, and they all ran off. I was surprised that the stone did not shatter its bones, but it was a long throw, and I was glad to see them gone, Henriette even more so. It was late afternoon and still several hours before dusk would be settling on us, and Henriette looked worriedly toward the sun.

"Do not be concerned," I told her. "We have several hours more of sunlight. Those wolves are gone. They will not be back."

She nodded, but apprehension tugged at her mouth as

she was uncertain about that. It took over another hour of walking and without any sign of those wolves before she was back to her previous cheerful self.

"I had never seen wolves before," she confided. "I think I was more afraid of their sight than even when my neighbors set fire to my cottage. And the way they looked at us!"

I kept thinking of those wolves also. The stone that I had thrown must have weighed over two pounds, and with the force that I used, the wolf that I hit with it should not have been able to run off with its pack. And the way they had stared at us with their eyes shining with a malignancy that was foreign in the other wolves that had attacked me. But they were gone now, and I tried to put them out of my mind and exhibit the same good spirits that Henriette was showing.

—⚜—

We walked until late into the night. Even though I did not need fire to see, I lit a torch that I fashioned with a tree branch and cloth from the rags that Henriette had previously worn so that she could see better. When we settled at last upon a grassy area, I made a fire, and then Henriette pleaded with me that I open one of our bottles of wine for us to celebrate. "It is not often that we get to stare down a pack of hungry wolves," she said, her face lit up by both the fire and an infectious smile that made me smile also. "And to hit a wolf from over fifty *ells* with a stone is reason enough to celebrate!"

I relented and opened up one of the bottles, amazing Henriette with how I was able to do so without a corkscrew. While she drank several sips of wine, she confessed to me that even though she had been in the employ of a beer hall she had had very little alcohol in her lifetime, adding that this was the first time she had tasted wine. After what could have been no more than a glass, she started showing the signs of being tipsy and soon afterward fell asleep. I covered her with my cape, then took the bottle from her and finished off the wine.

I watched over her for several hours, but the weariness from the wine and not having slept since I rescued Henriette from that burning cottage finally caught up to me and I drifted asleep also. Before too long I was visited by the same dark, troubling dreams that I had had previously. In the background was that same ruined castle reeking with its evil, and as with my other dreams, it appeared to beckon me. Right before waking I heard Victor Frankenstein's voice calling me his magnificent creature.

You have done well so far, my magnificent creature. Soon you will be with me.

I bolted upright expecting to see Victor Frankenstein whispering in my ear. But he wasn't there. No one was. My cape had been thrown aside and Henriette was gone.

A panic overtook me as I jumped to my feet searching for her. All I could imagine was that those wolves had snuck into our camp and had dragged her away. Whatever it was that Frankenstein had put in my chest pounded as I ran wildly looking for any signs of Henriette.

I had to be calm. I told myself this. If I was going to find Henriette I had to be calm. I forced myself to stop my running, and instead concentrated on whatever night sounds I could hear. Straining and holding my breath, I listened until I heard faint, ungodly noises off in the distance, noises that didn't seem possible to be coming from animals known of this earth.

I raced toward those noises. After I had run a mile I saw them. At first they were little more than shadows. As I moved closer I could see that they were of human form and they were naked. Four of them men, one of them a woman. Their bodies were thin and sinewy, and they crouched so that they faced away from me. The way their backs were hunched gave them a feral quality that sent a shiver up my spine. As they heard me approach, they turned toward me. From the deadness in their eyes, the starkness of their features and the wet blood shining on their lips, I knew these weren't men and women, but vampyres. I saw also that they had been crouching next to a living being. Although her face was hidden by their forms, I recognized the clothing. Henriette.

"Away from her!" I yelled. "Leave her or I will kill you!"

One of them, a male vampyre, seemed particularly amused by this. Presumably he was their leader, and he turned to face me. I noticed a thick welt showed on his hip.

"You will not do so," he said in a voice that dripped of ice and death. The other vampyres moved quickly to surround me.

"Why wouldn't I?" I demanded.

"The same reason that we did not slay you while you slept. Because we both serve the same master."

"That is not true!"

"Of course it is." He smiled at me though his eyes remained lifeless. "Only Satan's darkest arts could create a being like you, as he created us. I am curious, what type of being are you exactly?"

Henriette stirred on the ground. She was still alive. I raced over to her and was prepared to strike this vampyre down, but he stepped aside with a quickness that surpassed my own movement. I kneeled beside Henriette to soothe her. Their marks were upon her neck. As I tried to comfort her, she groaned softly.

"It is because of you that we took her," the vampyre told me while I tended to Henriette. "We were content to feed on the wayward traveler and lost soldier, but your brazen stealing of those young girls sent angry hunting parties into the forest. We had to move deeper into the forest ourselves to avoid them, and have found far less to prey on here. I am curious. What have you done with all those young girls that you stole?"

I did not bother to answer him. Henriette was stirring fitfully on the ground. Her eyes were closed, and her face looked pale in the dim moonlight.

"It is too late for her," the vampyre told me. "Because of her beauty, we chose not to drain her of all her blood, but to instead make her one of us."

I tried desperately to wake Henriette from whatever disturbed dream she was engaged in. The vampyre laughed at this, as did several of his companions. Henriette opened her eyes. When I saw the deadness in them, I knew she was lost to me. She made a horrible guttural noise, and sprang forward to attack me, but was still too weak and her attack was feeble. Her eyes closed and she collapsed back to the ground.

"This is unfair," I cried. "I was supposed to rescue her. She was supposed to live a good life in Venice. This is unfair!"

"Much is unfair," the vampyre said, amused.

The pain that seized my heart was as horrible as the guttural noise that had escaped from Henriette's lips. I tilted my head toward the pale moon and bellowed my agony at it. The other vampyres laughed at this. I sprung to my feet and turned to them in a murderous rage.

"I should kill you all," I swore.

"You could try," the lead vampyre said, his eyes darkening to the color of coal as he smiled at me. "You are of greater size, and most likely greater strength. But we have strength also, and a quickness that would most likely surprise you. Also there are five of us, soon to be six. But if you are successful and are able to kill us all, who would tend to your companion? Unless of course you wish to kill her also. If you do, now would be the easiest time as she is still very weak and in another hour she will be like us. All you would need to do is thrust your fist into her chest and rip out her heart. If you wish to do so none of us will stop you, although it would be a shame. I am so looking forward to ravaging her body once she has fully become one of us."

He had said this as a jest to mock me, but I realized this was the only way that I could save Henriette. If I left her, she would become a detestable night creature like these others. In life she was pure and innocent, and I could not leave her to become something vile. With my heart as heavy as stone I dropped beside her. Before any of the other vampyres could react, I struck my fist into her chest. A gasp came from her, but as I ripped out her heart, a peacefulness settled over her features.

"You are a fool," the vampyre hissed at me.

"Leave me or attack me," I demanded as I spun around to face them with Henriette's heart still clutched in my fist. Their leader stood relaxed while the other vampyres continued to circle me, moving like shadows as they did. At last their leader spat on the ground with contempt. "It would not be worth the effort," he said. "We would most likely choke on your blood." With that he turned and ran off with the other vampyres following him.

I dug a grave for Henriette and placed her body within it. After that I fashioned a marker for her grave out of loose stones.

I knelt by her grave and prayed for her forgiveness.

CHAPTER 14

I grieved by Henriette's grave over the next four days. The vampyres did not return, and I was left undisturbed.

When she was alive, Henriette had been an anchor holding me to the promise of being something better than I was. During our brief time together not only did I find myself enjoying her companionship and good cheer, but thoughts of bringing her safely to Venice had occupied my mind and kept my obsession for vengeance at bay. Henriette had made me feel human again. When I was with her I would frequently forget about my hideous appearance and often envision myself as Friedrich Hoffmann. But I had failed her, just as I had my dearest Johanna. Now that Henriette was gone, I was once again consumed by my desire for vengeance toward Victor Frankenstein, and once again felt that terrible pull on me to travel southwards.

I could no longer think of myself as something human, but only as an abomination. It was my actions that created the environment that allowed Henriette to be accused as a witch, and I was the one who led her to a nest of vampyres. I should have recognized those wolves for what they were. I should have known they were a different kind of creature from those that had attacked me earlier. How could I have failed to keep watch over Henriette after that? Although it was never my intention, I was the reason for her damnation, and perhaps also Johanna's. If Frankenstein was responsible for Johanna's murder as I suspected, would it have happened if not for me?

When I left Henriette's grave, I surrendered myself to the

urge that was pulling me south. I thought of what that vampyre had told me. How we both served the same master. Perhaps he was right. When I recounted all the evil that I had been responsible for since my transformation—from my noxious skulking through the homes of innocent men and women, to the fear that I created and saw so brightly in that young girl's eyes, and finally, Henriette's horrible fate—perhaps I had been serving the Devil without realizing it, and the goodness that I had earlier believed I still held from Friedrich Hoffmann was only illusionary. But I did not feel any of that goodness anymore. All I felt now was wretchedness.

I traveled aimlessly, letting that urge pull me where it wanted. When I came across a waterfall that would have delighted me when I was Friedrich Hoffmann, I felt nothing. Same with the other sights and sounds of nature. Colorful birds, wildflowers, ancient trees—no longer did any of these sights affect me. All I could feel was an ever-growing thirst for vengeance, and the overwhelming need to locate Victor Frankenstein.

One evening while dusk was approaching, I came across a satanic mass. The mass was being held in a clearing by a large rock that had a curious shape similar to that of a human head. Two trees grew on the top of this rock, appearing as if they were horns. I watched as several dozen figures hidden in black robes called out for Satan to join them, then as a goat was brought out and fed consecrated wafers.

A young girl was next carried out by several of their members. They held her down and stripped her of her clothing so that she lay struggling naked among them. When one of these black-robed figures showed a large curving knife to the sky, I realized that they were planning to sacrifice this girl, and I stepped out from my hiding place and ordered them to release her. I had my own hood off my face so that they could fully see me and fear me. They turned toward me, surprised by my presence, and then they fell to the ground kneeling in supplication. The one who had held the knife spoke.

"Oh Dark Lord, you have come as we have begged you to." He dared to look up at me, his face hidden under his black robe so that all I could see were his eyes shining with a mix of fear and delight. "We are your most humble servants. Once hearing how you have been traveling the country, we assembled here from a great distance to bring you forward so that we may serve you."

I said nothing as I took in this peculiar scene. So I was to be confused by them as Satan. Fine. I did not much care. Even with the hood covering his face, I could see this man who had addressed me lick his lips.

"We brought a virgin for you," he said, his voice trembling with nervousness. "We were about to sacrifice her for you. Would you like us to go through with the act? Or perhaps you would rather enjoy her first?"

The young girl could not have been much older than fourteen. She was so thin, just a wisp of a child, her legs and arms like broomsticks. Although they had released her as I demanded, she lay on the ground too terrified to move

"Where did you take her from?" I asked.

"A small village. Not too far from our own city of Innsbruck."

"Clothe her! She is to be brought back to her home. She is not to be harmed. Do you understand me?"

He nodded, although his eyes showed his disappointment. The girl was helped to her feet by the two members who had previously held her down, and they now helped her with her clothing. She looked like she wanted to flee, but was too paralyzed with fear to do so.

"Do not worry, child," I told her. "You will be brought home safely. I promise you that."

I turned to the leader of this black satanic mass. "Why are your people waiting? I want her travel to commence now!"

"Now?" he asked glumly. "But your lord, it will be dark soon and it is a hard two days travel."

"I see that you have torches. Your people can use them."

He nodded without much enthusiasm, and ordered two of the Satanists to take her. They didn't like the idea, and they tried arguing that they had traveled all this distance to be in my service and that they did not wish to leave me now. I ended their argument by bellowing at them to do as they were being asked. For a moment they both looked like they might expire where they stood, but once they regained their composure they nodded meekly.

"Make sure you bring enough food and water for her," I said. "I wish her to be made comfortable."

Again, they nodded with their eyes downcast. I watched as they gathered up supplies, and once they left with the girl, I ordered the other Satanists to remove their robes.

They did as they were commanded and stood naked in front of me. I was surprised to see that they were an almost even mix of men and women. The men all seemed to be either thin and bony or plump; none of them had the type of physique to indicate that they labored for their livelihood. Most likely these were bankers, lawyers and bureaucrats. Or perhaps noblemen who were provided incomes without ever needing to work. A grin wrinkled my face as I imagined how some of them might even be members of the clergy. The women among them seemed younger as a whole, and more attractive, but the softness of their bodies also showed them to be of the same privileged class as the men.

The Satanist who had held the long curving knife and who had first addressed me was of the thin and bony variety. He was perhaps fifty, and had a long scrawny neck that showed a pronounced Adam's apple. His face, like his body, held little flesh.

"Your lord," he spoke, his eyes showing his eagerness to please me. "We have brought a throne for you, and much wine. Would it please you to be seated?"

As I looked at him and the rest of the Satanists, a heavy weariness fell over me. At that moment, the thought of sitting down appealed to me, as did drinking enough wine to allow me to escape my thoughts. I told him to bring their throne, and the wine.

Half a dozen of them rushed off, and when they returned they brought back a wagon that was being pulled by a team of donkeys. These men proceeded to unload a great wooden chair that was covered with satin cushions. This chair would have been far too big for me when I was Friedrich Hoffmann, or any other man or woman, but was the proper size to hold me now. They struggled as they carried the chair to me. While they did this, other members removed wine barrels from the wagon.

I sat in this chair and it fit me well. One of them had filled a large golden goblet with wine, and had handed it to me. I drank it quickly and the goblet was refilled. Other Satanists built a fire. The goat was slaughtered, and I watched as they roasted it over the flames.

Their leader approached me, the one with the pronounced Adam's apple.

"I hope all is satisfactory," he said. "I apologize that the virgin we brought was not to your liking. Do you desire any of our women to pleasure you?"

The women all came forward to show themselves, their faces bright with anticipation and eagerness. I emptied my goblet and held it out for it to be refilled.

"Right now all I want is to sit and drink wine," I said.

"If instead you would like us to bring back younger girls for you, or even young boys—"

My eyes flashed as I growled at him that I wished for now to simply enjoy the wine. I was finding him equally as detestable as I had found Victor Frankenstein's honored guest, the Marquis. But the wine was dulling my thoughts and my senses, and I did not care how much I detested him or the others as long as my goblet was refilled. If they wanted to idolize me and pamper me, let them. As I drank more wine, the noise around me softened and the sights blurred. I barely noticed as the women danced naked around me.

CHAPTER 15

At first I was only going to stay among them long enough to make sure that that young girl was brought back safely to her home, but as the days blended into a week, I soon grew accustomed to being kept blissfully drunk. When the supplies began to dwindle, the Satanists sent out several of their members with their wagon to bring back finer foods and more wine for me. I became content to let them indulge me as they wished. The wine dulled the grief I felt about Henriette, although not so much for Johanna. Nothing seemed to be able to dull the aching hole I felt in my heart for my beloved. But the wine did help in abating the urge that pulled on me. If they wanted to keep filling my goblet and feeding me food, who was I to stop them? Besides, maybe they were right in idolizing me. It was the darkest and unholiest magic that breathed life into my new form, and perhaps I was also under Satan's spell when I performed my skulking and thieving. Maybe they saw me for what I truly was, even if I hadn't fully recognized that myself.

Their leader tried to ingratiate himself to me, sidling up to me every chance he had, making one wretched proposal after the next. Mostly I ignored him and drank my wine and ate the food that they brought me. But I detested him nonetheless, as I detested all of them. Whenever I would think of that poor girl who was stripped of her clothing and whom they were going to sacrifice, I would be hit with the impulse to squeeze their skulls into pulp. But those impulses would be fleeting, usually forgotten by the time I finished drinking my next gobletful. Still, though, I took a perverse pleasure in debasing them. After almost two weeks of keeping them naked, their leader worked up the courage to ask me if they could put their robes back on.

"It has become very uncomfortable," he admitted. "With insects biting our exposed flesh and dirt getting into uncomfortable areas—"

"Not now," I said, feeling my coarseness rising. "For now I demand that my loyal subjects engage in a copulation contest, the winners of which will receive my blessing."

I paired them off. There were two more men than there were women, so I paired their leader with a plump man whose skin was the color of boiled ham. I told the plump man that he would be the husband, and the leader—the one with the scrawny neck and bony body—that he would be the wife. Then I ordered them to commence, and they all did with a fervor that was terrible to witness. But I tried not to pay attention to them. For the most part I was able to ignore their grunts and squeals, and instead focused on the wine and on the drunken blissfulness that it provided me.

After an hour their noises showed more pain than pleasure, and I could sense them stealing looks toward me in the hope that this contest would end soon. I laughed inwardly at the wretchedness of this, and told them that I would announce at my choosing when the contest would be finished.

"If I detect any lack of fervor from any of you," I bellowed, "you will feel my wrath as no man or woman has ever before!"

That caused all of them to engage themselves more passionately, and soon the sounds that came from them were as if they being tortured, but I just closed my eyes and tried not to listen. Every time I was about to relent I thought of that young child that they had stolen to sacrifice, and instead I would fill my goblet with more wine. Perhaps at some subconscious level I wished to be done with them and hoped they would all expire from this activity, but it wasn't until the next morning that I stopped them. None of them had expired, but they all looked in great pain as they lay collapsed on the ground.

The winners turned out to be the plump ham-colored man and the thin bony-necked leader. They both had to struggle to get to their feet, and they looked as if they were in agony as they stood bow-legged in front of me. I had them turn around and bend over before I would give them my blessing. Then I staggered to my feet and booted one of them, then the other. My heart just wasn't in it, though. I was beginning to feel some pity toward these detestable persons, for I sent each of them flying less than ten feet. They both lay on the ground groaning miserably, but I had failed to cripple or injure either of them seriously, for within minutes they were both hobbling to their feet and thanking me for my blessing.

I told all of them then that they could put their robes on.

I then sunk back onto the throne they had constructed for me, and felt every bit as detestable as I found them. In my extreme cruelty, I had debased myself as much as I had them. Was there really any difference between myself and these devil worshippers? I laughed sourly over how fitting it seemed that they should be worshipping me. One of them crawled over to me to refill my goblet—a chore that I had had to undertake myself during the malicious physical activity that I had put them through. As I emptied this wine down my throat, I accepted that I had sunk to a level where I was no better than them.

It took my followers several days to recover from my cruelty, but during this time they still crawled about as needed to fill my needs. I do not think I ever felt more detestable as I realized how I deserved them every bit as much as they deserved me.

One evening as they were roasting a suckling pig for a feast they were preparing for me, their leader approached me with the idea of building a temple in my honor.

"We have the resources to bring workers here," he continued. "The trees here would provide all the timber that is necessary, and all the other materials could be brought here. We had so hoped that if we came to this sacred spot that you would appear, and we could build on this spot a temple befitting you!"

Usually I ignored this person, but in the low state I had sunken into, I grunted back how fortunate it was that I had stumbled upon them here just as they had arrived.

"Oh, we arrived here four days before you were drawn here by our devotion."

I stared at him confused.

He tittered, adding, "We knew if we were persistent in our devotion you would come to us, and you did."

"You had other ceremonies here?"

"Each night," he said, quite pleased with himself.

I tried to make sense of what he was telling me. "You made other sacrifices to me?"

"Of course, your lord."

"Human or animal?"

"Young virgins each night, similar to the one that you had us release. You would have been so pleased if you could have witnessed them. How young and supple these girls were, and how they screamed before I cut their hearts out. We knew their screams and our devotion would draw you to us at this most sacred and secret location, and it did!"

The wine had dulled me to where it took several minutes for me to fully understand the evil that he related to me. Once I did, I looked from him to the others. These were not just ridiculous men and women who were bored with their bourgeoisie existence and were now playing as devil worshippers. These were murderers of the worst kind. People who thought nothing of ending the lives of four innocent young girls. As corroded and debased as my soul might have become, I had not yet sunk to their level for I felt a sickening anger over what they had done to their victims. But I was not going to be the one to spill their blood.

"You have proposed an excellent idea," I said. I watched as this despicable man's face brightened with pride and vanity, and I added, "But this is not the place for my temple. I have a preferred location for it."

I told him where I wanted him and the rest of my followers to build this temple, and I gave him directions back to where I had encountered the vampyres. I knew the vampyres would still be hunting those grounds. Let them feed well and be the ones to drain these murderers of their blood. It seemed fitting. They wanted so badly to serve Satan, then let Satan's dark servants get to know them intimately.

"You do not have to leave now," I said. "We may have our feast first. Then you and the rest of my devoted followers will head to that site and wait for me there. When I arrive we will plan my temple together."

He was so enthralled that I had accepted his idea that it left him speechless, and all he could do was nod enthusiastically like an imbecile. When the pig had finished roasting, they brought me a plate, and as I ate my food and drank my wine I barely paid attention to their boisterous celebrations, nor as they packed up and departed into the night so that they could head to where I was sending them. Straight to a nest of vampyres.

For the first time in several weeks I was alone, and I found myself relieved to be free of their presence. I stayed seated on the throne that they had built for me and only left it to pour myself more wine. Over a course of several hours I emptied the last remaining barrel, and then later drifted into a drunken sleep. Fortunately the wine kept my mind too clouded to pay attention to any of my dreams.

CHAPTER 16

When I awoke the next morning and found the devil worshippers gone, I had a fleeting hope that the last several weeks had been nothing more than a fantastic nightmare. But that hope dissipated as I realized I was sitting on the throne that they had constructed for me, and saw the empty wine barrels littering the ground, as well as the pig carcass from the previous night's feast. Still, I enjoyed the solitude, and was glad to be free of them. I sat for several minutes listening to the sounds of the forest—birds and frogs chirping their melodies, the wind rustling through the leaves, animals rustling about in the underbrush—and as pleasing as these sounds were, after a short while I still strongly desired to flee this place and the loathsome memories that persisted there. I pushed myself to my feet, but before leaving I searched the area until I found four freshly dug graves. I then smashed my throne so that I could construct crosses from the pieces, and used the crosses to mark the graves. After saying prayers for each of the unfortunate children that lay under the dirt, I once again surrendered to that irresistible urge that I had been desperately trying to ignore, and let it pull me where it wished.

As my travel continued over the next half dozen days, the trees of the forest thinned, and I soon began entering desolate valleys and striding across rockier terrains. It wasn't long after that that I could see great mountain peaks off in the distance, and only a few days later that I came across a large and pleasant body of water that I would later learn was Lake Geneva. Following the banks of this lake, I reached the outskirts of the city. In my attempts to avoid the citizens of Geneva, I roamed the hills surrounding it, and ended up overlooking a popular promenade. This must have been a Sunday, for many families were strolling the promenade dressed in their finest clothing.

I stayed hidden on that hill and watched as these families paraded together; husbands and wives walking side by side, with the wives' hands invariably lightly touching their husbands' arms, and their children following behind them. After spending weeks with those detestable devil worshippers, I sat spellbound watching these good and gentle folks, and witnessed only expressions of happiness and contentment on their faces. At first this soothed me, but before too long these sights caused me to long more than ever for Johanna's gentle touch on my arm. It seemed so utterly cruel that the two of us could not be parading together with all these other happy people. I was about to quit this hill and my observing of these perfectly normal families before jealousy consumed me, when by happenstance I spotted them. An older man walking arm in arm with a young woman who, given her age, must have been his daughter, except that with her blue eyes and golden hair and gentle features she bore no resemblance to him. Behind them walked a young man of around twenty and a child who could have been no older than six. These two bore a strong resemblance to this older man. All three of them—the older man and what must have been his two sons—had thin, narrow faces, and high foreheads as well as strong aquiline noses, and they walked with what could only be thought of as a stately bearing. These three also bore a striking resemblance to Victor Frankenstein, so much so that I knew they must be related, although I could not see any cruelty or malevolence in their eyes or mouths. As I watched them I fought back an impulse to rush down from my hiding place and confront them. Instead I followed them back, unseen, to a grand house situated on the western banks of Lake Geneva.

I soon learned that they were in fact related to Victor Frankenstein. The older man was Frankenstein's father, the two boys were his brothers, and the young woman was supposedly his cousin, although from the lack of any physical resemblance I guessed that she had been adopted. Upon this knowledge I was seized with wicked thoughts; thoughts of using torture to force them to divulge my enemy's location, or even murdering one of them to draw my enemy out from wherever he was hiding. I was ashamed of these thoughts, and assumed they were brought about by the torment that I had felt earlier over my transformation and longing for Johanna. It was possible that these were good and innocent people. I saw no evidence from their bearing or expression to convince me otherwise, and I was content to spy on them and learn what I could about Victor Frankenstein.

Over the next several weeks I hid among them. Whenever I could I would spy at them through windows and eavesdrop on their conversations, and when their house was empty, I would climb an outside wall so that I could slip undetected through an open window. Once inside I would search through whatever letters I could find. I soon became convinced that they had no idea where Victor Frankenstein had gone off to, and that they were also goodhearted and charitable people. I further decided that they had no knowledge of their relation's evil activities. From what I could tell, the father, Alphonse Frankenstein, believed his son was merely studying medicine at the University of Ingolstadt, and was greatly concerned that his son was not responding to any of his letters. I also learned that the young woman, who was named Elizabeth Lavenza, had indeed as a small child been adopted by Alphonse and his departed wife during an act of kindness while traveling in Italy. This young woman, Elizabeth, believed herself to be intended for Victor Frankenstein, and that they would someday be married. I could not understand this for she appeared to be a gentle and good person, and all I could imagine was that Victor Frankenstein must have used his dark magic to bewitch her also.

Once I came to the conclusion that they could not help me find Victor Frankenstein, and that watching them any longer would be a fruitless activity, I left them and gave myself up once more to the invisible force that seemed intent to pull me southwards. I have since read the lies that Frankenstein recounted to Captain Walton, and of all of them none were more calculating and egregious than that I had murdered his youngest brother, William, and had caused a servant to be blamed for the murder by placing a locket that William had on his body within this servant's clothing. I can only imagine that Victor Frankenstein told this as one last cruel attempt to mock me—to accuse me of committing the very same act that caused me to be executed for my Johanna's murder. When I left Geneva, Frankenstein's young brother, William, was alive and well. What fate befell him later, I could not say.

The terrible urge that pulled on me sent me heading toward the great mountain peaks south of Geneva. Before long I was scaling these peaks, and doing so as easily as if I were a mountain goat. Even though it was now summer, I was climbing cliffs of ice and trudging through snow. This went on for days, and I soon began to wonder if I was being driven to an icy grave, for I could not imagine life being sustained in these conditions. I was still wondering why I was being sent to travel to such an inhospitable environment when I saw it.

The ruined castle.

The very same one that had haunted me so.

CHAPTER 17

I stood breathless, the ruined castle within my view. It lay high upon a treacherous cliff of sheer ice, and had the same menacing quality to it that it did in my dreams. For a long moment I remained paralyzed, unable to breathe or even move, and then all at once as if waking from a dream I gasped in a lungful of air and came back to life. And then I was racing across the glacier toward this castle.

The cliff was well over three hundred feet high and the ascent to the castle ran almost vertically. Often I had to strike my fist through the ice walls of the cliff in order to gain a hand hold so that I could continue climbing upwards. At times I thought I would drop to my death, but eventually I reached a level area and saw that a more passable path wound down the opposite side of the cliff. This path was better suited for man, and was littered with what looked like recent wheel and animal tracks. The surface was almost entirely of dirt and rock, with only small amounts of ice present. Even with the more stable surface, the path looked steep, and would be difficult for most men to navigate. A warm flush of excitement heated my skin as I thought what these recent tracks could mean, but I tried to remain calm.

I followed this path to the top of the cliff, which led me to a small stable situated behind the castle. I wasn't surprised to see the team of donkeys that were housed within the stable, nor the wagons that were also held there. Donkeys would have little trouble navigating that path, at least during these summer months. Once winter arrived this path would be impassable for either beast or man. The fact that the donkeys were alive and seemed to be in good health meant that the castle was indeed being inhabited as I had surmised, even given its apparent ruined state. My pulse raced quicker and a fury filled my mind as I imagined my enemy, Victor Frankenstein, so close.

I was barely aware of my surroundings as I strode to the main gate of the castle. Malignancy dripped so thickly from the stone walls that I could almost taste it in my throat. I did not know how I knew Frankenstein would be there, but I knew that he would, just as I knew that he had somehow summoned me to this godforsaken place. I trembled as I stood by the gate. Images of Johanna and her sweet smile and the way she would blush when I would steal a kiss flooded my mind. I thought about the life we were supposed to have together and all that I had lost and all that was stolen from my dear Johanna, and I burst through the gate roaring in fury, my heart in agony as if it were being torn apart.

The hall that I had stormed into held several craftsmen who were working to restore the castle to its former grandeur. I eyed them quickly but none of them were Frankenstein and he was all that I cared about, so I paid little attention as they fled the hall. I stood where I was, bellowing my rage, knowing that it would bring Frankenstein to me.

And it did. He wandered cautiously into the hall with a curious look upon his face. I raced toward him with every intention of throttling the truth from him regarding Johanna and Friedrich Hoffmann, but as I neared him I dropped to my knees, helpless. With my head bowed I told him in a guttural whisper that I was there to kill him.

"H-How is this possible?" he asked, his voice excited with fear. "How is it that you can talk?"

I groaned miserably at my situation. Here he was, my most detested enemy, less than an arm's length away and I was powerless to grab hold of him. I could not understand this.

"Why wouldn't I be able to talk?" I growled futilely at him.

My stare lowered to the marble floor. It took a great effort for me to look at him, and all I felt was shame as I saw that he had recovered sufficiently from his fright and now showed only that haughtiness that I despised so greatly.

"You shouldn't be able to talk, at least not this fluently, for you have barely the brain of a one-year old."

I laughed at that, but stopped abruptly as I saw a cruel, calculating glimmer in his eyes.

"Why is it that you wish to murder me, my pet?" he demanded, his voice soft but snapping at me as if a whip.

"Because I suspect you of murdering my betrothed, Johanna Klemmen, and arranging for me to be accused and executed for that crime. All so that you could gain access to the brain of an educated man."

His eyes widened and his sickly white skin drained of whatever color it possessed. For several long moments he seemed incapable of speech. When he was able to find his voice again, he asked me who I thought I was.

I cast my eyes down again and told him that I was once Friedrich Hoffmann.

"This is remarkable, truly remarkable," he muttered excitedly. "I never would have dreamed that you would possess your past intelligence. My most wondrous creation, I could not possibly express to you how exciting this development is, or how surprised I was to see you in such attire, or to be speaking such to me. How about your memories? How much do you remember from your past life?"

I forced myself to look up and meet his eyes. "I remember," I said. "I remember that a villain slipped a poison into my ale at the beer hall so that I collapsed unconscious in an alley. I remember the next morning how I was awoken by a mob, and that my beloved Johanna's locket had been placed on my person so that I would be accused of her murder. I remember my execution, every blow that the executioner made. I remember them in detail so that I may return the favor someday."

Frankenstein stood stroking his chin, a sly look slowly forming in his eyes. "You are right of course about my using Friedrich Hoffmann's brain as material in constructing you," he said at last. "But I believe you are being unfair with your other accusations. You could not possibly have any support- ing evidence to accuse me of these deeds. Is it not reasonable that I only took advantage of your execution to gain access to the material that I sought? Could not my involvement con- sist simply of bribing the executioner for your body so that it would not go needlessly to waste, and that I had nothing to do with the events which led to your being accused and convicted of this woman's murder?"

"Are you saying that you are innocent of my charges?"

He pursed his lips as he studied me. "I am not saying one way or the other," he replied mockingly, "for I do not have to. But I am curious why you believe me guilty of these deeds."

I looked away from him and pressed my lips firmly together so that I could avoid answering him.

"Answer me, my pet."

I tried, but I could not keep from answering him. It was as if I were being compelled by some unknown power to speak, just as I had been compelled to travel to this cursed place.

"I know how you murdered Charlotte," I said. A feeling of utter disgust welled within me for betraying Charlotte, but I was incapable of resisting Frankenstein no matter how hard I tried to keep my lips pressed together.

He raised an eyebrow at that. "Who is Charlotte?"

"You call her Sophie."

He trembled with excitement as he asked me why I believed he murdered his Sophie.

"You had her drugged. She was murdered as she lay unconscious, and her head removed from her body."

"I did this?"

"You hired a villain to do this deed for you."

"Is it not possible that I instead hired someone to procure me the material that I sought, believing that it would come from a dead body, and that I had no knowledge of this crime of which you speak? But never mind. How do you know this?"

I struggled to keep from telling him, but it was useless. "Charlotte told me." I heard myself saying this as if the words had come from someone else entirely.

"She has intelligence? Is that what you are telling me? That she is capable of conversing? Oh, my dear pet, this is absolutely delightful. And it explains so much, especially why you tried to hide your improvement from me back within my laboratory. I had wondered often about that. What exactly did she say to you to make you act that way?"

"She warned me to hide my intelligence from you."

"How did the two of you converse? She has no larynx, so speech is not possible for her."

"We silently mouthed our words to each other."

Frankenstein's eyes shone with malevolence as he contemplated this. Soon he could barely contain his grin. Others had slipped into the hall, and Frankenstein ordered one of them to retrieve Sophie for him.

"How is it that you control me?" I asked.

Victor Frankenstein cast me a disdainful look. He was anxious for Charlotte to be brought to him, and he was consumed with his thoughts on that and did not care for my interruption, but he answered me anyway, telling me that it was due to the nightly rituals he performed on me.

"Not only did these rituals raise you from the dead, but it made you my obedient slave, and you should be showing me more gratitude than you have been. Enough of this! And stand up already. I do not wish to have you kneeling by my feet. Not now, anyway."

I got back onto my feet. As I stood I towered over Frankenstein. I had the strength to crush him, but I was incapable of it. As much as I longed to reach for his throat so that I could squeeze the life out of him, I was helpless to act on my desires. He seemed to sense my thoughts and flashed me an annoyed look, but did not bother saying anything to me about it.

Charlotte was brought into the hall. She still rested in the same bowl that she had been in before, with several inches of milky liquid filling the bottom of it. At first her face showed the mask of imbecility that she used to hide her intelligence from Frankenstein, but as she saw me, first surprise and then alarm flashed in her eyes. I mouthed the words *I am sorry* to her.

Frankenstein took her and stroked her scalp, all the while staring at her mockingly. Charlotte looked even more frail than last I had seen her, her eyes more deeply hollowed and her skin appearing as if it were dried parchment paper. She tried to keep up her pretense, but she knew something was wrong and soon her expression showed her terror.

Frankenstein raised her so that she could clearly see his lips.

"My dear Sophie," he said, mouthing his words slowly. "You could not believe my surprise in learning what a devious creature you are, pretending as if you were nothing but an imbecilic novelty, when in fact you hold true intelligence. I am disappointed in you after all the hours in which I have petted you and let you suckle on my finger. The question I have for you, my dear Sophie, is why did you act in such an ungrateful manner? But first, answer me, are you capable of hearing words or only reading lips?"

Charlotte was too afraid to answer him, and Frankenstein in his impatience took hold of her earlobe and twisted it. Her skin, being so dry and fragile, ripped off in Frankenstein's fingers. This only enraged him more, and he took hold of the stump that remained and pinched it. It was heartbreaking to see the way Charlotte's face became rigid with pain. Frankenstein demanded again that she answer him, but she was incapable of doing so.

"Hand her to me," I implored.

My words broke through the petulance that held Frankenstein. He smiled cruelly at me and handed me Charlotte, announcing how he would not think of keeping two dear companions as us apart.

I mouthed my words to her, turning away so that Frankenstein would remain ignorant of what I was saying.

I am so sorry. I could not help myself from betraying you. The black magic that he deployed on me while I was his prisoner has left me powerless to resist him, otherwise I would have torn him to pieces instead. I am so sorry.

She favored me with the most heartrending smile I had ever seen.

My dearest Friedrich, how could I blame you for another man's cruelty? But I do ask a great favor of you. Please end my misery. I implore you.

A terrible thickness settled in my throat. I attempted to wrinkle a smile toward her but failed miserably.

Must I be your executioner?

Friedrich, my dear friend, I know this is a terrible burden that I am placing on you, but I beg of you. I cannot stand this. If you still hold any warm feelings toward me, please perform this one last act of kindness.

From out of the corner of my eye, I could see that Frankenstein was trying to follow our conversation. Amazement showed in his expression as he raised his gaze to better observe me.

"Are you actually weeping tears for this thing?" he asked incredulously.

"How do I end her life?"

"My pet, or should I say, Friedrich, for although you are my servant, I wish to think of you more as my partner. This mercy toward this thing that you believe you feel is not real. It cannot be. For you do not have a soul. How could you? You were constructed out of material, so how could you have a soul?"

I trembled as I again asked how I could end Charlotte's life.

"This is ridiculous," he stated, his eyes darkening with annoyance. "Friedrich, these fine sentiments that you believe you have are imaginary. They are simply remnants remaining within your brain from your previous existence. But they will fade. Ignore these false feelings now, my friend, for they are worthless."

"How do I end her life!" I demanded, my voice a harsh bellow.

A change fell over his eyes, from petulance to amusement. "Never let it be said that Victor Frankenstein cannot be magnanimous," he said in a cloying manner. "You wish to be a slave for now to these false sentiments, fine. If you remove her head from the bowl, she will die. Very painfully, I suppose, and over the course of several hours."

"There must be another way."

"A more humane way?" His lips crept up to make his smile even more vindictive. "You cannot smother her for she does not breathe, at least not in the way that we do. I suppose you could crush her skull. Go ahead, Friedrich, perform this ridiculous act of charity if you insist."

I dreaded that this would be his answer, but I could not see any other way. I placed the bowl on the floor and gingerly removed Charlotte from it. I mouthed to her how sorry I was, and she smiled and mouthed back to me that she would forever be grateful to me. I squeezed my eyes tight and after saying a silent prayer for Charlotte's soul, crushed her skull in my hands as if it were little more than a papier-mâché mask. Her remains crumbled into dust, and I placed them in the bowl.

Is this what I have become? A creature who can only save the innocent by ripping out their hearts or by crushing their skulls? I tilted my face upwards and roared.

Chapter 18

"Are you done yet?"

With my chest heaving, I turned toward Frankenstein. His words had barely registered on me. He shook his head sadly to show his disappointment.

"Friedrich, you are clinging onto these false sentiments as a way to convince yourself that you are still a man, but once you let go you will find that you have evolved into something much better. A superior being. A being of intelligence and cunning, as you previously were, but of much greater size and strength and without the curse of morality and conscience to weigh you down."

"Is that all you have to say to me?" I asked, my voice raw and inhuman.

He smiled thinly at that. "You intend to be stubborn. My friend, I will give you time to understand the truth." He hesitated, his smile turning impish. "Or is it that you wish to hold your grudge against me?" he asked. "That you desire only to blame me for the fate that Friedrich Hoffmann suffered, as well as that woman's? What was her name again? Johanna Klemmen? Would it satisfy you if you could ask her directly what happened to her?"

He stunned me with those words as severely as if he had struck me with a hammer. An iciness filled my skull as I stared at him, and I could not keep from trembling as I asked what he meant by that. "You have not transformed my Johanna into the same horror as you did Charlotte?"

His smile turned secretive as he considered me. "No, my friend, I have not. I will explain myself in due time. First let me give you a tour of our Temple of Nature, and later my cryptic words will make more sense to you."

He led me from the hall into a corridor, and as he did he explained that they were in the process of restoring the castle as well as readying it for a great drama that would commence on the first of November and would run for a hundred and twenty days. As we walked down the corridor we passed workmen who glanced fearfully at me, as well as a guest of Frankenstein's who looked at me only with curiosity and amazement. This guest appeared to be of the same sort as the devil worshippers that I had encountered; an older man, who, given his manner of dress and from the way he held himself, was wealthy, and, from the air of superiority that he exuded, had been born into his wealth. He showed the same cruelty and haughtiness in his expression as Frankenstein. While the two exchanged looks, the guest did not bother saying anything, nor did he join us.

"The first of November is still many months away and the necessary work should be completed by then," Victor Frankenstein continued, his words rushing out excitedly, his skin flushing a deep pink. "At least I pray so. There is still so much work to be done, but none of this would be possible if it were not for you. The drama that we will be presenting here will be art of the greatest kind. Sadly, it will only be a crude adaptation from a brilliant philosopher, for presenting the work precisely as written would be impossible, but I still hope what we present here will be transcendental." He stopped himself as if he were remembering something. "My dear Friedrich, you have met this author. The Marquis visited my laboratory in Ingolstatd when we believed you had the simple intelligence of an infant. And you, in your deviousness, were able to eavesdrop on us and understand our conversations without our knowledge. The Marquis will be amused when he hears of this! Although I will never hear the end of it, for he was convinced then that you held intelligence!"

Frankenstein had led me into a semicircular room, and he stopped his speech so that he could watch my reaction to what he was presenting to me. In the center of this room sat a decorative throne that had been elevated four feet above the floor with its back resting against the wall so that it overlooked the room. Marble columns rose to the ceiling from both sides of this throne. Hooks were attached to these columns, and from these were hung cat-o'-nine tails and other whips, and evil-looking devices at whose purpose I could only guess. Embedded halfway up each column were iron manacles, and the purpose of these was easy to surmise. They were meant so that a victim could be chained between these columns and left suspended in the air.

Scattered about this room were couches and chaise longues that were covered with satin cushions. The room had the feel of an evil amphitheater, and I guessed this was where the play that Frankenstein had mentioned was to be performed. What was most striking and what filled me with the greatest sense of loathing were not the columns decorated with their instruments of torture, but a mural that ran fully around the room and held a height of at least eight feet, with the figures within it painted to be life-sized. This mural reflected what was at first glance a pleasant ballroom scene of men in their elegant attire and women in their fine ballroom gowns waltzing happily together. But if you looked more closely you could see a glint of wickedness shining in the men's eyes, as well as hint of horror shading the women's complexions. I tried to look away from this strange painting, but it was as if I were compelled to stare at it, almost as if I were afraid to look away from it.

"You are enjoying the mural?" Frankenstein asked, obviously pleased with himself. "This is my own contribution to the Marquis' brilliant work, for he could not possibly have divined a mural of this sort, as will become apparent to you over time. But I am quite pleased with it. Here, let me show you more."

He led me to one of what were a half dozen closets attached to this room. Frankenstein opened the closet door, and inside, it was furnished with a couch similar to those scattered about the main room, with other whips and evil devices hanging from the walls. When we stepped out of the closet, I stopped, confused. The mural appeared to have changed subtly, the men's faces all the more sinister, the women's faces registering a touch more fear. I also imagined that their positions within their waltz had changed, as if they had taken several steps during my absence. Frankenstein seemed pleased by my confusion, but only asked that we continue our tour.

"The other closets are all the same as the one I showed you," he said. "But let me show you the dining room, which is, sadly, still under construction."

Frankenstein took me to an adjoining room, which was to be the dining room. Workmen were hanging rich red tapestries and painting the walls and crafting an ornamental molding made of ivory along the edges of the ceiling. A great oak table sat in the middle of the room, and scattered about this table were fine armchairs with fat leather cushions. There was nothing overtly sinister about this room—at least not like the amphitheater that I was shown—but it still filled me with a sense of loathing. Perhaps it was that an evil permeated the interior of this castle as completely as if it were air, and that it would chill me wherever I went within these castle walls.

From this dining room, Frankenstein next showed me a set of private bedrooms, all of which were still under construction. Even with the canopied beds and the other fine furnishings, these rooms filled me with the same sort of revulsion as the dining room and amphitheater.

"The living quarters for my guests are on higher floors," Frankenstein confided to me. "These chambers are to be used for the drama that we will be performing. Come, there is still much I desire to show you."

He took me to a stone staircase that led into the bowels of the castle and what appeared to be a dungeon. Workmen were assembling a complex set of gears and machinery across eight pillars that stood in a row, all of which had manacles attached to them. Frankenstein stopped to admire this. He pointed out a chain and told me that when it was pulled the victims who were secured to each of these pillars would be murdered simultaneously.

"All done through different means," he giggled. "Garroted, stabbed, set on fire, shot by darts and other exquisite forms of death. It will be a thing of beauty."

"What do you mean the *victims who are to be chained to those pillars?*"

He fought to contain another giggle, but otherwise did not answer me. Instead he moved hurriedly to an iron door and pulled it open. He stood eagerly by this open door waiting for me. On entering this chamber I found cages filled with young girls, none of which could have been older than twenty. I stared at them dumbfounded. There could have been several hundred of them, and as I looked at their horrorstruck and pitiful expressions, I saw that were even younger children among them, both boys and girls.

"These are to be the players in our drama," Frankenstein told me.

I stared at him as dumbly as I did those poor prisoners, Frankenstein's words not yet sinking in.

"Of course, I will be playing a role, as will several of my guests. But these will be the star players of our production, and none of this would have been possible without you, Friedrich."

I could not understand what he was saying, and as he saw my bewilderment his expression grew exceedingly wicked.

"We stole them when you were terrorizing the Saxony and Bavarian provinces," he explained, his voice slicing me as sharply as if it had been a dagger. "All of these thefts were blamed on you. Without your help, Friedrich, we would never have been able to procure the players that we need for our drama."

I closed my eyes and imagined the feverish state that I had been in when I stole into those cities under the cloak of darkness and skulked about their citizenry, almost as if I were little more than a puppet being manipulated by an invisible hand. I understood then.

"It was your black magic that sent me into those cities and villages, and made me act I did," I said, my voice rumbling out in a soft echo.

"Of course," Frankenstein said.

I looked at the faces of these young girls and children as they stared back at me, horrified. All I could see was innocence and purity.

"These are who you will be murdering on those machines?" I asked, not quite believing that any man, no matter how evil, could do as Frankenstein was suggesting.

"Some of them will play that role," Frankenstein said. "Others will be assigned their own special roles, all of which they will play out as demanded. In the meantime, they will be well-fed and kept healthy, and their innocence will not be breached. We need all of them to remain virgins leading up to our drama, although none will remain virgins for very long after it begins."

He chuckled at that.

The full magnitude of what I had seen and what Franken-stein was telling me began to sink in. The murdering ma-chines, the devices for torture and other evil. And with utter disgust I understood the unwitting role that I played.

"This is not a temple of nature," I spat out, "but a tem-ple of depravity!"

Frankenstein's eyes darkened and his smile lost some of its luster. "You are wrong, Friedrich," he said. "In nature, is there such thing as murder and rape? If a tiger wishes to kill another animal, does it not just do so? If a male beast wishes to make use of a female of its species, or any other species that it is stronger than, does it not just overpower it and do as it wishes?"

"We are not animals."

"But we are, Friedrich. With all of our pretense of being something greater than that, that is all we are, and our drama will be representing the ultimate truth of nature, and not the hypocrisy of man and his supposed high morality. In Paris right now, under the guise of piety and God, the sanctimo-nious fiend, Robespierre, is each day sending hundreds of innocent men and women to their death by the guillotine and unleashing rivers of blood so great that they have had to build special gutters to contain it. In Spain, for such alleged crimes of heresy, hundreds of innocent men and women are tortured and murdered each day in ways every bit as barbaric as what our play will call for. The few lives that we will be sacrificing here for our little drama will be a drop of piss compared to the oceans that these civilized nations pour out."

"What you are saying is nothing but an excuse for a few wicked men to act out their sickness. Why should these in-nocents be the ones to suffer? Why not you?"

"Because, Friedrich, in nature the strong prey on the weak."

"Then let me use my greater strength to rip the limbs from your body. That would make a fine statement concerning the power of nature."

A shadow passed over Frankenstein's eyes as he looked at me. The smile that he had been favoring me with faded and a dullness settled over his features.

"This has grown tiresome," he said. "I had such high hopes for you. You, of all creatures, who must be so detested simply for your physical appearance by these same men and women whom you insist on bleeding tears of compassion for. With these fine sensibilities of yours, I suppose there is little chance that you will ever again be able to speak to Johanna Klemmen. To do so would be too offensive to your virtuous nature. It is a pity that she will forever be lost to you."

Chapter 19

Frankenstein's words had the calculated effect that he planned. I could barely contain myself as I stammered out for him to tell me what he meant by this.

"But my dear Friedrich, I am afraid it would upset your sensibilities if I were to do so."

"Tell me!"

He shrugged, and in an air of utter casualness he told me how he had obtained Johanna's brain as material, and had been keeping it preserved using the same liquid that he used to keep Charlotte living.

"Why would you do this?"

"Why?" A malicious glint showed in his eyes as he considered me. "No particular reason. I was able to procure the material and thought it would be amusing to reunite two lost lovers, although I never imagined that memories and intelligence would be retained in your brain or hers. But now it would be a fascinating experiment to test whether love is indeed spiritual or merely brought about by physical attraction, for if I were to bring back your lover, would she be able to look past your hideous appearance and still have deep affections for you, or would she simply be sickened by your sight?"

I did not say anything. My eyes cast downwards toward the stone floor. I could not have met Frankenstein's cruel eyes for any purpose, for my strength bled out of me as surely as if my jugular had been severed.

"Well, Friedrich, shall I sacrifice one of these young girls so that you may be with your beloved Johanna Klemmen once more? Or would that act be too repulsive for you?"

For a long moment I could not answer him, then my voice barely a whisper, I uttered, "Do as you wish."

"No, Friedrich, that is not good enough. You must decide or I will dispose of your beloved's brain and she will be lost to you forever. If you need to, you can rationalize your decision with the knowledge that you will be saving one of these young girls, for none of them will be surviving past the end of our drama. But I will not be sacrificing one of these girls for this purpose unless you are a willing accomplice. One last time, do you wish me to bring Johanna Klemmen back to you?"

God help me, I nodded my assent.

"That is not good enough. I need to hear your words."

I forced myself to meet his eyes and all the maliciousness that they contained. "Do what is necessary to bring Johanna back to life," I said, my chest aching so that I could barely stand it.

He nodded solemnly. "I will do that, Friedrich. But no more of your lectures, and no more of your false nobility. Now which one of these should be made into Johanna Klemmen?"

I shook my head. "I do not care. You choose," I said.

The smile that next twisted his lips chilled me as nothing before had ever done.

"No, my friend," he said, "you will choose her, but it will be done in a most sporting way."

———

Frankenstein assembled the rest of his guests in the dungeon, and I was surprised to see that they consisted of women also. In total, his guests comprised seven men and four women. I was also surprised that the Marquis was not among them, although I later learned that they expected his arrival within two weeks' time. As with the guest that I had seen ear-lier, they all appeared to be of wealth, and they all clearly shared Frankenstein's perversity. There was little difference between them and the devil worshippers that I had encoun-tered, except that I was powerless against them, as I equally was against Frankenstein.

While I stood helpless, servants brought out the prison-ers for me to look over, and I was compelled to do so both by Frankenstein's black magic and his implied threat of dis-posing of Johanna's brain if I failed to cooperate. It all had such a surreal nightmarish quality to it as I was forced to look into these poor girls' faces as they wept with fear and misery, all the while Frankenstein and his guests tittering with amusement and making wagers over which girl I would select. Frankenstein in his evil even had the young children brought out for me to look over. Several times I wished to die when these innocents begged me to rescue them. But I knew I could not, and overpowering in my mind was the de-sire to be reunited with my Johanna, as grotesque a manner as this reunion would be brought about. In the end I chose one of them.

"When will this be done?" I demanded.

Frankenstein looked at me slowly as if he were going to comment about my tone, but in the end chose to ignore it. "Not for several weeks," he said, his own tone peevish. "I need to travel to London first to consult with others who have knowledge that I need since the operation of placing a brain in an otherwise undisturbed body is very different from my constructing a being from material, as I did with you, and I will also not be leaving until after the Marquis arrives. So be patient!"

With that the party broke up. Frankenstein and his guests quitted the dungeon, and I was compelled to follow them. I wandered about as if I were in a spell, at times sinking into deep despair over my unwitting role in this atrocity and my inability to help these innocent prisoners, at other times anxious over the prospect of once again being in Johanna's company. The tearing that was done to my soul over this was something awful, and it was with surprise that I found myself drawn back to that evil amphitheater. When I looked up and saw the ballroom scene, I stumbled backward, disoriented, for it appeared to me as if the couples within the mural had danced halfway across the room. None of them were where I remembered them. Other details also seemed new to me. One of the men now held a dagger behind his back; a woman's mouth froze in the beginning moments of a scream; lines of terror showed in other women's faces. As I stood transfixed at this mural and puzzled over these changes, one of Frankenstein's woman guests approached me.

"Later this will become much more interesting," she told me.

Earlier I had been introduced to all of Frankenstein's guests, and this one was a viscountess from an extraordinarily old family. If I had not known the evil that lay in her heart, I might have mistaken her for an attractive woman who perhaps bordered on beautiful, but even still, I might have detected her icy countenance. I did not bother to respond to her attempt at conversation. Instead I moved my gaze back to the painting.

"Victor mentioned that he constructed you to be quite well endowed," she said with a snicker. "Or in his words, large enough to make any stallion envious. I wish to see your cock. Show it to me."

Frankenstein's hold on me extended to his guests. I was powerless to disobey her, and as if unseen strings were controlling my hands I opened my cape and lowered my trousers. She made a gasping sound and then proceeded to amuse herself with me. I stood there helpless, unable to move or command my hands to throw her away from me. Soon one of Frankenstein's other female guests joined her, while several of the male guests entertained themselves by watching. Perhaps it was my imagination, but it seemed to me as if several of the waltzing couples within the mural were now smirking at me.

I was required to join them for dinner, and Frankenstein seated me next to himself. Their conversation quickly grew tedious as it revolved around the same tired themes that Frankenstein had brought up to me earlier. I attempted to drown them out by drinking glass after glass of brandy. They were too involved in their pontificating to notice, and after a while the brandy did help to dull out their voices. After dinner ended, I found myself drawn once more to the amphitheater, and this time there was no denying that the scene had changed. The couples were no longer happily waltzing, but now the men were displaying an animal savagery as they ripped the dresses from their partners and threatened their throats with the blades of knives. I blinked several times, wondering if I was seeing what I thought, or if the brandy had left me so intoxicated that I was merely imagining this sight.

"My friend, you are beginning to understand the nature of my mural."

Frankenstein was smiling patiently at me. I did not wish to ask him anything but I couldn't help myself.

"How?"

"If I can bring you back to life, why not a painting?"

A sickening feeling filled me as I turned my gaze back to the mural and the evil it represented.

"They are very sly devils," Frankenstein said. "They will not move while being watched. Later, at midnight, they will, but not now."

I knew Frankenstein wished me on my own accord to come back at midnight so that I could watch how the actors within his mural would play out their drama, and for that reason alone I avoided returning to that room that night, as much as my morbid curiosity begged me to. Instead I took several bottles of brandy to the bedroom that Frankenstein assigned to me. The bed that he had constructed for the room was almost twice the size of a normal bed, and so it fit me, as did the silk sheets and enormous blankets that he had specially made. Frankenstein also had a special armchair constructed to hold my size, as he also did for the dining room. I sat in this chair and drank the brandy that I brought back with me, hoping that it would dim the self-hatred that raged within me. I tried to remember my life when I was still Friedrich Hoffmann. I tried desperately to think of Johanna, but my thoughts kept reflecting back on the horrors that I had experienced since awakening inside of Frankenstein's laboratory. My execution and rebirth as a hideous abomination, poor Charlotte existing only as a disembodied head, wolves turning into vampyres, devil worshippers and their human sacrifices, this castle and the utter depravity within it, complete with a living mural of horrors. My thoughts eventually slowed as the brandy succeeded in dulling my senses, and a heavy weariness fell over me. I closed my eyes and before too long, mercifully, I fell into sleep.

This time Frankenstein's black magic did not invade my dreams, for there was no purpose since he had already compelled me to join him at his castle. Instead I found myself drifting into a peacefulness that seemed almost foreign to me. At first it was as if I were being rocked back and forth within a gentle breeze, and then I saw Johanna. She smiled contentedly at me, with only love and admiration in her expression, her long yellow hair flowing down her back. But she was naked, and I blushed deeply and looked away, and saw that

I too was naked and my body was that of Friedrich Hoffmann's.

"Friedrich, my darling, there is nothing to be ashamed of. I have waited so long to visit you. Please look at me."

Johanna's voice was as a balm soothing my soul. I turned toward her and found myself instantly lost within her gentle hazel eyes. She held out her hands to me, and I grasped them hoping to never have to let go of her.

"I have missed you," I said.

"As I have missed you, my darling. I have tried so many times to visit you previously, but something strong and oppressive kept me from doing so."

My eyes misted quickly, but I did not dare to let go of her for even a second to wipe away my tears.

I said, "When I think of what was done to you—"

"Please, Friedrich, don't."

"But the villains responsible must pay for what they did. The crime that was committed against you is too horrible to even think of. It must be avenged! Justice requires it!"

"Let God worry about punishing the guilty," she said. "All I care about is being able to spend eternity with you, and I am afraid that that will not be happening."

Her own eyes had become liquid with tears and her smile troubled, and it tugged at my heart to see her like that.

"Do not be concerned," I said. "I will be seeing you soon, and then we will have the rest of this lifetime together and eternity afterward."

She did not say anything, but her brow turned more troubled and a darkness clouded her delicate features.

"Embrace me, Friedrich," she said in a hushed whisper, "for I am afraid that this will be our only opportunity."

I embraced her, our naked bodies touching, my hands resting on her slender hips, her own arms wrapped tightly across my back. I had never felt more joy than I did right then, but also an intense sorrow as I realized that this would soon end. Johanna began to weep, and she buried her head in my chest, her tears hot against my flesh. I tried to soothe her by stroking her hair and whispering sweet words into her ear. After a while she stopped her weeping. She pulled away slightly so that she could look into my eyes.

"Friedrich, you must leave this castle," she said.

"I cannot," I said with despair. "The fiend, Frankenstein, has employed black magic to hold me here."

"You must find a way, my darling. And you must also find a way to rescue the girls that they're imprisoning here, for the plans that they have for these innocent girls are even more vile than what was done to me."

I could not answer her. I knew she was right, but I did not know how to do what she was asking.

She kissed me then on my lips with an intensity that made me dizzy. As she pulled away, she whispered to me, "I am so afraid of losing you, Friedrich. Please do not be lost to me."

I wanted to answer her, to promise her that she would not lose me, but before I could I was jolted awake, my body having crashed to the floor from falling out of the armchair where I had fallen asleep. As I lay on the floor, I did not want to believe that I had woken, and I desperately tried to hold onto the dream I had of Johanna, but her image proved to be as elusive as vapor. She was gone, and as I looked at my hands, I had to accept that I was no longer Friedrich Hoffmann, but once again a repulsive abomination. I began to weep as I lay where I had fallen, and felt the full weight of all I had lost sinking down my heart.

Later, when I could stop weeping, I cursed Frankenstein yet again for all that he had stolen from me.

CHAPTER 20

Each day I would be left alone to wander the castle as I pleased. My enemy was too busy with his plans to pay much attention to me, as were his guests, and his black magic kept me imprisoned within the castle walls as surely as if bars had been placed across the main gate, although even without his spell I did not know if I could have left with the prospect of seeing my Johanna being brought back to life.

The morning after my arrival I found myself once more drawn to that evil amphitheater. The scene had reverted back to show the couples happily waltzing across a ballroom floor with not even a glimmer of malice discernible in the faces of the dancers, and the women fully clothed in their fine ball gowns without any evidence of them having been torn off the previous night.

Later that afternoon I discovered illustrations that were made for the drama they were planning, and what I saw was beyond vileness, beyond depravity. I stared in shock at these sketches, and could not imagine any human mind designing such acts. It was hard even to imagine Satan himself dreaming up such evil. There were hundreds of these illustrations, but I could not view more than a dozen of them without feeling whatever was left of my own soul rotting inside of me. I tried to burn those damnable drawings in the fireplace, but Frankenstein's black magic compelled me to place them back where I had found them.

After seeing those pages I could not do nothing. I waited until the workmen left the dungeon, and then I snuck down there with the intention of freeing the prisoners that were being held, but Frankenstein's same evil spell prevented me from doing this. The keys to the cages were hanging on a nail in the wall, but when I tried to pick them up my arm fell dead to my side. Not seeing my form in the dim light, the young girls and children cried out to me, pleading to me to save them, but I couldn't no matter how hard I tried. In the end I fled the chamber, too ashamed to face these poor innocents.

That night I was required to dine with Frankenstein's company, as I was every night that I would remain within the castle, but as I had done previously, I drank enough brandy to deaden them to me and their voices became little more than a droning in my ears. After dinner I found myself once more drawn to the amphitheater, and the scene displayed upon the mural was similar to that of the other night, with the men cruelly ripping the women's gowns from their bodies, and in some cases, their knives drawing blood across their victim's faces. The fascination that this mural held for me disgusted me, and as tempted as I was to return at midnight I avoided doing so again.

I did not sleep that night, and I used those twilight hours to search more of the castle without anyone's knowledge. It was past daybreak when I found a secret panel that held Frankenstein's library of rare occult texts, but only moments later I heard noises of others within the castle awakening, and since I did not wish to have anyone stumble upon me and learn of my discovery, I placed the books back within their hidden compartment.

The next night, when the rest of the inhabitants of the castle were asleep, I returned so that I could read this occult collection undisturbed. The manuscripts were ancient, their bindings all of aged and cracking vellum, although with one of the books I had the thought that human skin was used, as well as blood instead of ink. I handled these books carefully so that their pages would not crumble apart in my hands. Several of them were written in Greek, others in Latin, and I could feel the evil emanating from them simply by holding them. It was a loathsome activity, touching and reading these books, and it took me four nights to complete my task. It was in the last of these books—the one that I believed had human skin as its binding—that I found the spell that Frankenstein had cast on me to make me his unwitting slave, but nowhere within its pages could I find a counter-spell. I was ashamed to realize that I was relieved by this, for it left me with no choice but to allow Johanna to be brought back to me.

This knowledge that I was a compliant if not necessarily willing participant in Frankenstein's plans filled me with a new revulsion that sent me reeling. I had been trying to believe that I was only an innocent prisoner within the castle walls, the same as the caged children; that since there was nothing I could do to save them, none of this was my fault. But was I secretly hoping that I would be left with no choice but to allow Frankenstein's plans to play out? Left to my own accord, would I be willing to sacrifice not only one of them but all of them if it would bring Johanna back to me? How could I be above their evil if I were secretly glad that I could not prevent it? These questions preyed on me, and sent me roaming the castle like a ghost. For the rest of the day I barely paid attention to where I wandered, or to the amused looks with which Frankenstein and his guests favored me. It was as if I were walking listlessly inside of a nightmare that I could not wake up from, and it was in this dark state of mind that I found myself back in the amphitheater at midnight.

Frankenstein and his other guests were already assembled there. It must have been a nightly ritual for them. And Frankenstein was right. At that hour the actors within the mural moved freely and without any care that they were being observed. Their movements were fluid and held an eerie quality, and the scenes that played out were every bit as inhuman as the illustrations that I had seen for Frankenstein's planned drama. The women all had their clothing torn off, and in some cases were dead, having had their throats cut so savagely that their heads hung as if by a thread from their bodies. The women who were still alive all had at least one or more of their limbs cut from their bodies, and blood flowed from them every bit as much as it would have from a living person, and it left a red stain spreading across the dance floor. When they opened their mouths wide to scream, no sound emanated from them and their screams remained trapped within that nightmarish mural. Whether the women were alive or dead, it did not stop the men from raping and sodomizing them in ways that earlier would have been unimaginable to me. Some of the men would turn to grin wickedly at us, others were too caught up in their bloodlust to notice that they had an audience. As each depraved act unfolded, Frankenstein and his guests applauded with an animalistic fervor, their own faces burning feverishly as if they were in a spell. As I watched, I found my own legs increasingly growing unsteady, and when the actors within the mural turned to acts of cannibalism I staggered out of the room before the swimming within my head sent me crashing to the floor.

I was only a few yards from the amphitheater when my legs gave out from under me, and I crawled desperately to find a dark corner where I could lose the memory of the images that I had seen play out on that mural and the sound of the enthusiastic applauding and cheering from Frankenstein and his guests.

I made my way into one of the boudoirs where the noises coming from the amphitheater were muted enough to where I could almost ignore them. An iciness ran through my body, my skin as cold and damp as a corpse's. I pushed myself into a sitting position and rocked back and forth as I grasped my knees, and kept telling myself that what I saw wasn't real, but only the imaginations of a madman.

Except that the acts that had played out on that mural were very much like the fates that were intended for the prisoners being held within the dungeon, and for some, what was planned for was far worse, at least according to the few illustrations that I had looked at.

If I could, would I be able to save them, even if it meant that my Johanna would be forever lost to me? And even if I remained powerless to stop Frankenstein from carrying out his atrocities, would the fact that I secretly wished to remain powerless damn my soul every bit as much?

But at least I was saving one of them from that cruelty. I tried to take solace from that, but failed miserably.

For the rest of my days in the castle I avoided the amphitheater, but nothing I did could stop those images from torturing me.

Ten days after that night, the Marquis arrived. He did not arrive alone; since Frankenstein intended to bring me to London with him, he arranged for a tailor and boot maker to be brought also to the castle so that I could be properly outfitted for my trip. All of them arrived together in the same carriage, which brought them to the base of the cliff, and a wagon pulled by donkeys was next used to bring them up the path and to the castle. I did not see the Marquis arrive, or even later that evening at dinner, for he had to rest after his arduous journey. I did however meet immediately with both the tailor and boot maker, neither of whom were allowed the luxury of claiming that they were too tired to commence their work. That afternoon the tailor measured me for a suit that I would wear under my cape, as well as a pair of gloves to hide the monstrous nature of my hands, and the boot maker did likewise so that he could construct for me a pair of leather boots. Both of these men shook noticeably as they took my measurements, as well paling even whiter than milk, but they did their work, and by the following afternoon they delivered to me my clothing and boots. Frankenstein commanded me to try on my new suit, and as I did, he nodded his approval.

"A proper gentleman," he said with a trace of a smile. "Wear this tonight for dinner. I would like the Marquis to see you like this."

I nodded my consent, since I was incapable of doing otherwise, and that evening I arrived for dinner as Frankenstein commanded. The Marquis was already seated at the table. He looked the same pompous, rotund creature that I had seen in Frankenstein's laboratory, except that his heavy jowls sagged more and his flesh appeared grayer around his eyes. His back faced the door and he did not notice me enter, but continued his conversation with several of the other guests about how fascinating he found Frankenstein's mural.

"The actors within it only seem to move when I look away," he said. "Although they have been up to much wickedness of late."

"Wait until midnight!" the Viscountess exclaimed excitedly. "They will not show any shyness in their actions then!"

The Marquis was about to respond to her when he noticed me, and instead stopped to nod in my direction. Frankenstein also then noticed that I had entered the hall, and commanded me to take my seat, which would put the Marquis directly to my right.

"I have you to thank," the Marquis said gravely. "Without your services we would not have been able find the players that we needed to perform my masterpiece. I viewed our actors earlier today, and they will be quite adequate."

I held my tongue. I knew Frankenstein had not made his threat idly to dispose of Johanna's brain if I showed any outrage over their intentions, and the fact was I was no longer sure whether I had the right to claim any moral superiority to them. The Marquis waited for me to answer him, and when I did not a thin smile showed on his lips.

"You do not approve of our intended drama?" he asked.

I chose my words carefully, and told him simply that I did not see the point of it.

"That is because you do not understand it," he said, an angry petulance entering his voice. "I was wrong before when I thought I perceived intelligence in you when I visited Victor in Ingolstadt. Clearly you are an imbecile if you cannot see the brilliance of my drama!"

Frankenstein laughed hastily. "Do not be offended, my friend. Friedrich still clings to his noble aspirations, but that will not last for long. And he knows only bits and pieces of what we have planned. He has seen some of our illustrations, and has surmised other aspects of your drama, but that is the extent of his knowledge. When he sees the work in its entirety, he will appreciate what we are doing."

I wondered how Frankenstein knew that I had viewed the illustrations. Had he spied on me? Or perhaps it was his dark magic that had compelled me to find them? The Marquis interrupted my thoughts by making a loud *harrumph* noise. His expression turned sullen as he picked up his brandy and sipped it. When he put the glass down, his eyes had darkened.

"I do not care whether this abomination of yours appreciates my work," he stated in a tone as dark as his eyes. "But I will be making him an actor within my play, and will be commencing with my revisions tomorrow. Does his cock work? That is all I wish to know right now!"

The Viscountess answered him, telling the Marquis how

she had firsthand experience that it did. "We put on an exhibition for the actors within Victor's mural, and I believe they enjoyed our show every bit as much as we do theirs!"

The Marquis chuckled at that and drank more of his brandy. This time when he put the glass down he smiled nastily at me, a hateful glint in his eyes. "In that case, my daemonic friend, I will be revising my drama to give you a starring role. But enough of that. Congratulations are in order. I understand that you chose one of the young girls to be your bride."

He waited for me to answer him, and when I failed to, his smile turned nastier and he continued, "A delightful creature, the one you chose. I paid particularly close attention to her when I examined all our prisoners earlier. Although at twenty years she did seem too ripe for my taste, but still quite pretty, even at her advanced age. Her rosy cheeks and yellow hair made me curious concerning what she had beneath her peasant dress."

With his eyes still intent on me, he ordered Frankenstein to send this girl later to his room.

"But we agreed that we would wait until November first, for when our drama is to begin—"

"Since she is not going to be one of our actors, her virginity is of no importance. I wish to spend the night sampling her. And I will be doing our imbecilic friend here a favor by training her in all forms of pleasure so that she will be better prepared for her wedding night."

"If you touch her I will kill you," I told the Marquis.

He laughed at that. "How? You cannot even keep me from doing this?" He stood up and struck me on the face. If I were in Friedrich Hoffmann's body, perhaps his blow would have drawn blood, or have even knocked me down, but in my current form it was little more than a tap. Still, I trembled with rage as I stared into his face, but Frankenstein's spell forced my hands to remain at my sides.

Frankenstein interrupted this scene, nervously imploring the Marquis to sit down. "I will be sending her on a long journey tomorrow in preparation for the transformation. My dear Marquis, it is best for tonight that she be allowed to rest. I am sure one or more of the madames here would be happy instead to oblige you tonight—"

"One of them? My God, are you insane? They are all approaching forty!"

Frankenstein hurriedly pulled the Marquis over to him and whispered into his ear. At first the Marquis looked annoyed and wished to argue with him, but in the end he allowed himself to be pacified. He turned to me and nodded curtly. "I apologize," he said in a stilted voice. "I can at times display a violent temper. Please blame my behavior on artistic temperament." He then turned to address the rest of the table and also apologized to the ladies sitting there for his outburst. With that he continued with his meal, although his mood had soured considerably.

Frankenstein called me to his side and whispered to me that it would be best if I left the table. "You should rest, my friend. We will be starting a long journey tomorrow."

I did not argue with him. I was glad to be free of them, especially the Marquis. On the way up to my room, I picked up more bottles of brandy, anxious for the blissful oblivion that they would provide me.

CHAPTER 21

The next morning Frankenstein arranged for the girl that I chose to be transformed into Johanna to be sent ahead to an isolated island off the coast of Scotland, as well as Johanna's brain, notes, instruments and other medical devices that he would be needing for the operation. He had, it appeared, rented the entire island for the surgery, choosing it for its proximity to England and its isolation. While I understood Frankenstein not wishing to be burdened with this girl while the two of us traveled to London, his shipping her off as if she were little more than any other piece of laboratory equipment troubled me, but I did not attempt to argue with him.

After those arrangements were completed, Frankenstein had a trunk brought down from his living quarters so that the two of us could prepare for our journey to London. The Marquis met him in the parlor and told Frankenstein that he would be hard at work on his revisions, but that he would have everything ready for the first of November. He turned away from me with only a faint acknowledgment of my presence and still with a malicious glint in his eyes. After that, Frankenstein and I departed the castle. We sat together in a wagon while a team of donkeys pulled us down the path and to the base of the cliff. On this side of the cliff was a small cabin and a stable that had been hidden from me when I had arrived weeks earlier from the other side. An attendant had a coach waiting for us. Once we were boarded and under way to Strasburg, I asked Frankenstein why the tailor and boot maker were not accompanying us. He looked away from me and peered off toward the icy glaciers.

"They have costumes and other work to perform in preparation for our drama," he said under his breath.

His tone and manner led me to believe that it was more than that. That those two, and perhaps all of the workmen and craftsmen employed at the castle, were never going to be leaving. That they were all going to be made unwitting players in the drama that was going to unfold.

Frankenstein appeared absorbed in his own thoughts, which suited me, since I did not care for his company. We did not speak another word together until we arrived in Strasburg and boarded the boat that Frankenstein had chartered to take us up the Rhine to Rotterdam. Once I had gained access to my cabin without any attention from the boat's crew, Frankenstein asked me to stay shut in my cabin during the day, and not to venture out onto the deck until the darkness of night had descended.

"I will bring you food and wine and whatever else you might need," he said, "but I am afraid that if the crew were to see you, even hidden under your cape, it would alarm them. Stories of a gigantic daemon kidnapping young girls could have reached this city."

I did not put up any argument. I did not much care where on that boat I resided.

Whether it was the travel, being free from that castle and its thick oppressive evil, or the cool, soothing air from the water, that night onboard the ship I slept deeply for the first time in over two weeks. While my dreams were not invaded by Frankenstein's black magic, they were troubling nonetheless, and as much as I had hoped for Johanna to visit she did not appear. I awoke from these dreams with an uneasiness that had burrowed deep into my soul and which I could not rid myself of no matter how hard I tried.

I was mostly left alone over the next several days, with my enemy only interrupting me to bring food and drink. During this time I tried to convince myself that all I had witnessed within the castle was only a fleeting nightmare that I had left far behind me, and I tried desperately to hold on to Johanna's image within my mind, but her face would invariably break apart only to be replaced by the shifting faces of the young girls in Frankenstein's dungeon, and I would see them clearly in all of their misery and despair. I would see them begging me to save them. And even when I would open my eyes, I would still be haunted by these phantoms as they would insist on lingering for a horrible few moments more.

When I would look out my cabin window I would see sights of nature that would have soothed and pleased me when I was Friedrich Hoffmann, but now only left me barren, and worse, for before too long I would make out those young girls' faces within rock formations and clouds. There was no escape from them, no escape from the terror that I had left behind. The worst was when scenes from that mural would play out in my mind, with the women within it being replaced by the young prisoners. I would at times pace my cabin as if I were a caged animal, at other times I would hold my head in my hands, but nothing I did would keep those loathsome thoughts from pushing their serpentine way through my skull. Every minute that I was held captive within those castle walls I had prayed for distant solitude, and now that I had it I could barely stand it.

The night before we were to reach Rotterdam, I stood on the deck and stared into the darkness. Alone, I tried to breathe in the night air in order to try to keep my torturous imaginings at bay. I was interrupted by the arrival of Frankenstein. He stood silently next to me, and I made no attempt to speak to him. We stood like that for several minutes before Frankenstein remarked that there existed a bond between us, a bond similar to that which existed between a father and a son. I laughed harshly at his comment, the noise escaping from me and sounding like little more than a dog's bark.

"It is true, Friedrich. For I crafted you and brought life into your dead form. I witnessed when you first opened your eyes. I cared for and nurtured you when you were helpless and had no strength to move. And while at times I am disappointed with your progress, I am excited about your potential."

I tried not to answer him but I could not help myself, his words enraging me.

"My father was a good and gentle man," I said. "He spent his life painting porcelain figurines, which only served to bring delight into people's lives. I assure you my father never dreamed of torturing and murdering innocent children for any purpose."

Frankenstein ignored the anger in my voice, and his own temperament remained calm, maybe even melancholy.

"Friedrich, you need to let go of these false sentiments that you insist on clinging to. What you were before was only a man. That person died, but what you are now, what I in fact gave birth to you as, is something far greater. You will understand this someday, as you will the purpose for the drama that we will be performing. It is far more than what you believe it is. Our drama seeks a higher truth, and will enlighten mankind in a way that no drama before has ever hoped to do. Give it time, Friedrich. You will see this, I am sure of it, and when you do you will have fully evolved into the superior being that I know is your destiny. I am sure that you will also then feel the same bond between us that I feel."

"If this bond between us truly exists, then free me from your black spell," I said. "Let me feel this bond without it being choked by your magic."

"There is no way to free you from my spell," he said. In the darkness, I saw the calmness upon his face as he stared out toward the river. "I wish I could free you from it, Friedrich. Not now, of course. Not while you are making this request sarcastically and wish only to rip my limbs from my body. But later. Unfortunately, I will never be able to do so."

I again did not wish to speak further with him, but I could not restrain myself.

"If you believe that these sentiments of mine are merely illusory," I said. "And that I am destined to be as black-hearted and devoid of conscience as you and the rest of your company, then why are you willing to bring Johanna back to me?"

My enemy paused before answering me. "To help you along the path that you need to take," he said. "Of course, I have other reasons. This is an experiment that I have longed planned to attempt, and it would be fascinating to see whether this woman's memories have been retained, as yours were, and how she reacts to you in your new form. But of utmost importance was to have you choose to have a young girl murdered to satisfy your own needs. With this step taken there will be no turning back and there will be little doubt that you will evolve as I have hoped."

"You would have murdered her anyway," I argued. "And in a far more sordid and horrible manner!"

Frankenstein shrugged halfheartedly. "Perhaps, but perhaps not. You cannot know for certain what would have happened. What if we decided not to perform our drama, and instead free the prisoners? Or what if the French army caught wind of what we were doing and sent troops to rescue them? No my friend, no matter how you rationalize this, you will be culpable in this girl's murder."

I brooded over this, for he was not telling me anything that I had not already been torturing myself over. Of course, he was lying about the chances that they might cancel their planned drama. They were hell-bent on seeing their plans carried out. The girl that I chose would be murdered in any case. But Frankenstein was right. I would now be responsible for her death.

A thought entered my mind, and I began to tremble. "Once you have brought my Johanna back to me, you cannot harm her!"

He nodded. "You have my word on that, Friedrich, although I believe that you will soon have little use for her."

"And you cannot bring her back to your castle! That madman there would incorporate her into his damnable play if you did!"

"Do not worry, Friedrich. I will not renege on my promise to you. She will be kept safe, and I will keep her away from the castle, at least during our performance, for you are correct of course. I am sure the Marquis already has plans to include her in the proceedings. But you are wrong about him being a madman. He is a visionary, as I have full confidence that you will eventually understand. Would it surprise you to know that the Marquis has acted as a judge in Paris, and that he has saved dozens from the guillotine? And that he has been persecuted for this?"

I bit my tongue to keep from remarking how the most cruel will at times try to wear the disguise of the heroic and the martyr to keep their true nature hidden. I did however ask him what it was that he had whispered to the Marquis after the man's petulant outburst at dinner the other night.

Frankenstein sighed heavily before telling me, "I reminded him that our guests not only shared our philosophy but were funding our enterprise, and that he should not insult them. I also made sure that he understood the deep affection I feel for you."

"Why is it that your spell appears to hold more power over me each day?" I asked. "There were times when I traveled through Saxony and Bavaria and felt only a dull pull on me, and was sure that I had free will over my actions."

"Certainly not when you were sent into those cities and villages," he said. "But you are right. The spell is like a parasite that grows inside of you. I wish that were not the case, but it is." He paused before adding, "I would also like to believe that your obedience is partially due to your deeper affections toward me, even if you are refusing to acknowledge it."

With that my enemy bid me good night. I stood where I was for several hours until the blackness of the night began to dissolve into a hazy grayness, and only then returned to my cabin.

CHAPTER 22

We left for London the same day that we arrived in Rotterdam. Frankenstein urged me to crouch as low as I could when we boarded the ship in an attempt to limit the attention that I would draw. He had every right to be worried about this, for I could not help but draw attention to myself—not only because of my massive size, but due to my manner of dress and the unseasonably hot summer weather. Anyone wearing the cape that I wore, especially with the hood raised to hide my face, would arouse curiosity. I could have suggested that I take a small boat myself to London, or even use that boat to later board the ship under the cover of darkness, but I enjoyed watching how Frankenstein's brow became ruined by consternation, as well as the way he squirmed whenever a crew member or fellow passenger stared in my direction and whispered into a companion's ear. In the end, no one approached us and we made it to our private cabin without incident. Frankenstein was perspiring badly by this point, and seemed to be reacting nervously toward every footstep outside our cabin door.

"I should have arranged other means for you to reach London," he said, his anxiety tightening his voice.

"Are you afraid that the crew might come to us and demand that I remove my cape and reveal myself to them?" I asked, taunting him.

He nodded, too consumed with worry to note the mocking tone of my voice.

"That would be a shame," I said. "For I might be compelled then to tell them of the young prisoners that you are holding within your castle's dungeon in Chamounix. As well as the plans that you have for them."

His eyes flashed as my words brought him temporarily out of his stupor. "And lose your dear beloved Johanna Klemmen forever?" he asked, his voice cutting as a scalpel. "I don't think so. But even if you were to try something like that, your voice would fail you, and would find yourself quite mute. But Friedrich, it is good to see this cruel streak in you, for it shows that you are making progress."

With that, he sat by a small table and poured himself a glass of wine, his hand shaking as he brought it to his lips. When footsteps sounded outside of our door he nearly spilled the wine down his jacket, but after a pause the footsteps moved past us.

"Once we arrive in London there will be nothing to worry about," he said.

"I am not worried," I said, a harsh grin wrinkling my face.

Annoyance pinched his mouth, but otherwise he ignored me and poured himself a second glass of wine. I had been crouching inside the cabin, for if I stood straight my head would have gone through the ceiling. I became weary of standing like that, and took a bottle myself, pulled out the cork with my fingers, and sat on the floor and drank the bottle as a baby would milk. It was more than an hour later, and after several additional glasses of wine, that Frankenstein recovered from his panic, and his familiar haughtiness showed once more in his eyes and on his lips.

"We fooled them, Friedrich," he said. "They were only within several feet of you when you passed them, and not one of them suspected what you are. The idiots!"

"Or maybe they did," I said. "Maybe they have guards posted by our door and are waiting until we arrive in London before arresting us."

This goading affected Frankenstein as I had hoped. Alarm crept into his eyes, and he had difficulty relaxing over the next eight hours of our voyage as he attempted to forget my words. I got little satisfaction from this, and soon I grabbed another bottle of wine, ignoring him. When the ship docked, Frankenstein had us stay holed up within our cabin for another hour so that the night would grow darker before we left. Even then, he opened the cabin door only a crack so that he could peer out and be sure that armed guards weren't waiting for us.

"They could have the guards waiting at the disembarkation point of the ship," I said. "That is what I would do if I were them."

In his nervous state he took this latest taunt of mine to heart. "Very true, Friedrich, very true," he murmured, both too drunk and anxious to think properly. He chewed on his bottom lip before his bloodshot eyes glanced up to meet mine. "Here is what you will do," he said. "I want you to climb from the deck down the side of the ship, and from there jump onto the pier. You can do that, can't you? And make sure nobody sees or hears you. Wait in the shadows for me. Once I have left the ship I will find you. Or you should signal me if you spot me first."

I nodded my assent and cursed myself. If I had kept my mouth shut, I would have been able to walk past the crew members with Frankenstein at my side, and maybe he would have then died from fright and I would be free from his damned spell.

Frankenstein left the cabin before me, then I skulked unobserved to the midpoint of the ship, and from there I climbed down a ladder and easily jumped so that I landed like a cat on the pier. There I waited until I spotted Frankenstein and I signaled for him as he had commanded me. His mood had brightened considerably.

"We did it, my friend," he exclaimed heartily. He reached up and clapped me collegially on my back as if we were best of friends. I gritted my teeth at this, but held my tongue.

"We arrived here without arousing undue suspicion. From this point on there will be nothing to worry about."

Sadly, I believed he was right. He arranged for a hackney carriage, and under the cover of night, I slipped inside of it without the driver being able to see much of my features. The seat groaned under my weight and the floorboards sagged. Frankenstein muttered that he was going to have to arrange for coaches from now on, but as the lone horse strained under the driver's whip, the carriage got under way.

CHAPTER 23

Frankenstein had rented the first floor of a rooming house near the Charing Cross section of London. We arrived in the pitch-black of night, with the carriage driver having to hold a lantern in order to see ten feet in front of his face. The street that the rooming house sat on seemed aptly named given its new tenant: Craven Street. After the carriage brought us to the address, Frankenstein pointed out the private entrance that the flat had, and told me that was why he had rented it. I stood in the darkness while the carriage driver struggled to carry in Frankenstein's trunk, and waited until he drove away before I entered the apartment. These ceilings were also less than eight feet high, and I had to stoop. Frankenstein didn't notice or care, and appeared to be in high spirits.

"This will be an exciting few days," he told me. "I suspect you have never seen anything like London before. While I will need you to stay indoors during the day, feel free to roam at night and see what you can of the city."

I had had more than enough of Frankenstein's company during the voyage, and I took him up on his offer. Before he could say another word I was out of the flat and moving fast to get away. A crescent moon showed in the night sky and provided little light, and the air was hazier than I was used to, but with my nocturnal vision I could still see well enough in what was close to blackness. Frankenstein was right. This was unlike any city I had yet seen. The buildings appeared haphazardly slapped together as if no planning was done, and the area more cramped than even in Ingolstadt. It gave me the impression of walking through a honeycomb. But it was the dirt and filth of the place that I noticed most. Garbage and rotted food had been tossed into the streets and it filled them with an inescapable stench. As I walked I noticed more rats scurrying about than I had ever seen in my life.

I had been heading toward Charing Cross, and I stopped at what I saw. In the open was a public pillory with a man bent over, his head and arms locked within the wooden structure. I heard him moaning miserably, and I walked over to him. It was too dark for him to see me, but I could see the anguish on his face, as well as the stains from the rotted fruits and vegetables that had been thrown at him.

"Why are you locked up like this?" I asked.

My voice surprised him, but he answered me. "They accuse me of stealing a loaf of bread and two pounds of mutton," he said, his voice a hoarse whisper.

"Are these accusations true?"

He squeezed his eyes closed and nodded as much as the pillory would allow. "Yes, the food was for my brother's widow. She has children and they are hungry. And, yes, I did steal what they claim."

I considered this for only a moment, and then I broke the pillory open to free him. Before he had a chance to thank me I was walking away.

I kept walking north, using the few stars I could make out in the sky to guide me. Mostly I made my way through narrow alleyways and streets, although at times I would come across small parks and gardens and buildings of remarkable grandeur. I was no more than a few miles from where I had freed that man from the pillory when I spotted five men standing together in the darkness. Somehow they sensed me and they moved quickly so that they surrounded me. They were big men, although nowhere my size. But each of them was over six feet tall and thick shouldered, and they held long knives. They reminded me of the wolves that had first attacked me when I traveled to Leipzig.

One of them addressed me. "Aye, mate. If you are going to pass, you got to pay our toll."

"What is your toll?"

He laughed at that. "Listen to his accent. A foreigner." This was said to his companions. Then to me, he said, "Your pig snout. That is what we collect, and that's why we are members of the Pig Snout Club. So remember that for when you tell stories of how you lost your pig snout!"

While I had studied English, I hadn't spoken or heard it much in my life, and I wasn't sure if I had heard right. "I do not have a pig with me," I said. "So I am afraid you will have to collect your snout from someone else."

"That's not how it works, friend. We'll collect the snout from you. From your own face, mind you. So stand still and be prepared to pay your toll. Or put up a fight if you wish."

They moved toward me, and it was only when they were a few feet from me and realized my size that they stopped. Once more they reminded me of those wolves, except with the men I felt no remorse over what I was going to do. They only hesitated briefly. I suppose they decided that even with my greater size, they were armed and there were five of them. And in the darkness they couldn't see me clearly enough to realize what they were going up against.

When the first of them stepped forward to stick me with his knife, I grabbed him by the arm and broke it as if it were a dried stick. Before he could utter a sound I lifted him over my head the way you would lift a sack of flour. He started shrieking then, but it did not last long as I threw him at two of his advancing companions. These two also cried out as they fell to the ground with their friend sprawled out on top of them, either dead or unconscious. The two remaining proved less courageous than the wolves had, and they both took several steps backward.

"Aye, Charlie," one of them cried out. "Was that you who screamed? What happened? Henry?"

"I think he's murdered Charlie," one of them on the ground cried. "And he's hurt us terribly."

The two standing snout collectors turned and ran. I could have given chase and caught them, but instead I approached their three helpless companions who were left on the ground and kneeled beside them. I took a knife from one of them.

"Maybe I should start my own collection," I said, and I placed the blade under his nose. All I needed to do was push my thumb against the back of the blade, and his nose would come clean off.

"Please, Cap'n, don't do that," he pleaded. "I got a mum and two sisters. Don't do that to me. We were just having our fun, that's all."

"How many noses have you collected so far? And do not lie. I know when I'm being lied to!"

He hesitated before telling me that so far he had only collected a mere four noses, and that two of them were only little beaks that together barely amounted to a full nose. He started blubbering then, and in his tears added, "But it was done for sport, Cap'n. We weren't out to cause any real mischief."

"Just a group of high-spirited gentlemen," I said.

"That's all we are, Cap'n." Then he was sobbing too hard for further words.

The thought of someone maiming innocent passersby for sport sickened me. He deserved to be marked for his villainy, and he certainly did not deserve the mercy that I showed him, for I broke the knife blade in my hand, and left him and his two companions with their noses still attached to their faces.

They were not the only villains that I encountered in the

darkness of London. That same night I had others try to attack me, some for sport who also gave themselves colorful names, others expecting to rob me. The same happened every night that I walked the dark London streets, even when I tried to walk along the banks of the Thames to avoid them. These villains that came from the dark to prey on the innocent seemed as numerous as the rats that I would see scurrying about, although none of them that approached me fared any better than the snout collectors.

It was our fourth day in London when Frankenstein showed up at the flat early in the evening before the sun had fallen. He had been spending his days consulting with other occultists and scientific researchers so that he could gain the necessary knowledge for his planned operation regarding Johanna, and had been too preoccupied in his thoughts to show much life during this time. That evening he was flushed with excitement as he announced that I would have to forgo my nightly activities, for he had plans to bring me to a special gathering.

"We will be leaving here at ten o'clock sharp, for we have an invitation to an exclusive club where you will be the guest of honor," he said nearly breathless.

"The Pig Snout Club?" I asked

He gave me a curious look, but did not bothering pursuing my dubious comment, and he soon left me to prepare for the evening's festivities.

By ten o'clock, Frankenstein was dressed in his finest clothing, complete with a red satin cape, and his skin was still burning a bright pink over the anticipation that he held for the gathering. A coach was waiting for us when we left the flat. The moon wasn't much more than a crescent and only a few stars were able to break through the haze of the night air. While Frankenstein had the driver hold his lantern so that he could enter the coach safely, he asked the driver to go back to his station when it was my turn so that I could slip in unseen.

While the coach drove away, thoughts rattled through my head of how I could get my enemy onto the London streets at night, for I knew villains were skulking about out there. Frankenstein would not last more than a mile walking in the darkness before one of these villains caved in his head with a club or stuck him through the heart with a knife. But there was nothing I could do to trick him into leaving the coach, and when I turned to throw him out by force, my arms slackened at my side and became dead things.

He sensed my movement and gave me a puzzled look. "Do you want something, Friedrich?" he asked.

"Only to know about the nature of this club," I muttered in defeat.

"You will see soon enough, my friend."

I sat back hating myself for my weakness. But I knew I had only been deluding myself. Even if I had the strength to push him from the coach, fear of losing my Johanna forever would have overpowered me and would have stilled me as surely as Frankenstein's black magic had. I sat back within my seat and brooded in my self-loathing.

CHAPTER 24

The coach followed along the Thames for several miles before turning down a narrow unlit street, then making additional turns on several more cramped roadways before coming to a stop by a stone wall. The driver craned his neck to look back at Frankenstein and to tell him that this was the address. "You're sure this is where you want to be let off?" the driver asked him.

"Yes, of course. Let me make use of your lantern."

The driver reluctantly handed over his lantern. Frankenstein held it as he left the coach, then stood with his back to the stone wall. I followed him but stood outside of the glow of the light. Seconds later a man wearing a black cape similar to mine stepped out from the darkness to stand next to Frankenstein. As he got closer to the light from the lantern I could see that he also wore a black mask over his eyes and nose as if he were a bandit. He did not say anything, but even with his mask I could see him staring intently at my enemy.

"We will be drinking heartily to our master's good health and rosy glow," Frankenstein uttered softly, and this costumed man nodded his assent at these words.

"Here, give this back to the driver," Frankenstein said hurriedly, handing me the lantern. As I returned it to the driver, his eyes grew wide as he saw my size from the glimmer of the light that the lantern produced, but he did not say anything, and with a lash of his whip sent the horses pulling his coach away. It was then that the man who had slipped out from the shadows to meet Frankenstein pressed in an innocuous fashion on several stones along the wall, causing a hidden doorway to unveil itself to us as a section of the wall swung out. The costumed man then led us down a steep and winding stone staircase, the ceiling of which was so low that even Frankenstein had to stoop to keep from grazing his head, and I had to walk nearly bent over. As we navigated down these steps, Frankenstein commanded me to lower my hood, as it would not be necessary where we were going.

Finally we reached the bottom of the staircase and entered a room that was filled with steam and the smell of sulfur, as if we had entered Hell itself. Red flames burned along the path we walked, and cages filled with fluttering bats hung from the stone ceiling. At the end of this room, our guide opened an iron door that was so small I had to get on my knees to crawl through it, and afterward found myself inside of a room that was considerably cooler than the steam-filled room that we just left. This new room held about a dozen people, most of whom were dressed in similar costumes to our guide. Some of these people were lying sprawled upon fur-lined divans, while others were standing. Our guide did not join us but instead left, presumably so that he could bring down other visitors who were able to tell him the same password that Frankenstein had.

This time I did not have to worry about scraping my head against the ceiling for it was over twenty feet high. The group of people rushed toward us, and one of them handed both Frankenstein and myself pewter goblets that were formed in the shape of Satan's head, complete with curved horns. Frankenstein whispered to me that members of the club all wore black capes and masks while guests wore what they pleased.

"He does drink, doesn't he?" this man asked.

Frankenstein laughed at that. "More than ten men. I've seen him empty many a bottle of wine and brandy without bothering to come up for air."

"Well, then, he should enjoy some good old English whiskey!" This man peered closer at me, his eyes squinting. "Remarkable, truly remarkable," he muttered. "And you built him yourself? I would have guessed that he had come straight from the bowels of Hell!"

"It was my handiwork," Frankenstein said, a smug smile curving his lips. "But Hell did play a role. It was Satan's power that breathed life into him. In his own way he is as close to Satan as we will ever get, at least in this lifetime."

"How did you bring him to life?" this man asked.

"A rare book I uncovered," Frankenstein said. "Over five hundred years old, and from this I was able to unlock the secrets of alchemy. And he is proof of it!"

"Is it . . . I mean, he, safe?" one of the other guests asked.

"Quite," Frankenstein said with a thin smile. "Right now he would like to do nothing more than to rip me to pieces, but he is incapable of doing anything other than being my obedient slave, thanks to the satanic magic that I employed. Isn't that true, Friedrich?"

I drank the amber liquid in my goblet before answering him, and the whiskey burned my throat. Once, Herr Klemmen and I drank cognac together to celebrate my betrothal to Johanna, but this beverage was stronger. I handed my empty goblet to one of the guests for him to refill it.

"Throttling you would be sufficient," I said.

My answer brought a vindictive glint to Frankenstein's eyes, but before he could say anything else one of the women club members commented about how strong I looked. "Could we have a demonstration?"

"Of course, madam," Frankenstein said with a polite bow, and he nodded toward two of the club members, both of whom with their round pear-shaped bodies and thick whiskers would have been in trouble if they ever ended up in the hands of the surviving members of the pig snout collectors. I grabbed them by the backs of their capes, holding them so that I also had a grasp of their jackets, and I raised my arms so that I lifted them straight up into the air. They sputtered their indignation over this, and were red faced by the time I dropped them back to the floor. Several of the other members were laughing at this demonstration, and these two men decided that it would be better to take it in good humor.

"Can you have him disrobe?" the same woman member asked. "I would like to see him naked!"

Several of the other members and guests murmured their desire for this also. I instantly regretted my throttling comment and gave Frankenstein a pleading look. His vindictiveness continued to glimmer in his eyes for a long moment, but it faded and he surprisingly shook his head.

"I am sorry, but Friedrich is here as a guest, as I am, and it will be his decision whether he disrobes."

More whiskey was handed to me and my hand shook as I drank it. I was relieved, but still hated that I had to feel gratitude to Frankenstein for not forcing me to debase myself in front of this group. I handed my once again empty goblet to the same member to pour me more whiskey. As I looked around the room I saw a few small statues and other artifacts that confirmed to me that these people liked to think of themselves as devil worshippers, or at least they liked to play that role. Maybe it was the whiskey, or maybe it was that I desired to show them what frauds they were, but I mentioned how I had spent over two weeks with devil worshippers. That got their attention. Even Frankenstein raised an eyebrow.

"This was in the Austrian forest. They were holding a black mass at the base of a rock shaped like the Devil's skull. When I stepped forward they mistook me for Satan, believing they had summoned me forth with their mass."

"What happened next?" one of them asked.

I was handed more whiskey. This time I only took a sip

instead of draining the pint that was held in the goblet. "They catered to my every whim," I said. "After a while I grew tired of it, and them as well, and I sent them to their deaths."

A few of them laughed nervously at that. "And how did you do that?" asked one of the pear-shaped men that I had lifted.

"I directed them to travel to where I knew a nest of vampyres would be waiting."

That drew more nervous laughter from them.

"The stories that this creature tells," one of them said. "Such an imagination!"

"Yes, such," Frankenstein agreed. "Next he'll be telling us that he's the dark avenger that London has been whispering about over the last three days. The one who supposedly has recently taken to roaming the dark London streets so that he can injure the villains and other such bandits waiting to prey on the good citizens of this city."

I was surprised that these types of stories were already circulating, and although Frankenstein said this with a thin smile, I knew from the hardness in his eyes that he suspected I was this person, as he probably also suspected that my story about the devil worshippers was more than simply my imagination.

I drank more of the whiskey, and was beginning to feel the effects of it. "The devil worshippers I met might have been despicable," I said as a scowl twisted my lips, "but at least they were sincere in their practice."

"And how so?" one of them asked with a chuckle.

"Human sacrifices, for example," I said, my voice breaking into a soft mumble. I looked away from them to stare instead into the bottom of my now almost empty goblet. "They were devoted, I will give them that. Despicable, but devout. They did more than stand about in the safety of a private club and drink whiskey."

The club member who had been filling my goblet with whiskey laughed at that. "While we may not perform human sacrifices here, we do more than just drink whiskey. This is only a meeting room. Let me show you more of our club."

He led us to the other side of the room and to a set of heavy red curtains, all the while talking excitedly to Frankenstein. When he got to these curtains, he reached into his cape and handed us hickory sticks and then beamed at us.

"Welcome to Satan's Paradise," he announced with a grin. "Nothing quite like this on earth, I guarantee you."

"What are these sticks for?" I asked.

"You'll see," he said.

Frankenstein pushed through the curtains first, and then I followed.

CHAPTER 25

We found ourselves in a large cavernous room teeming with club members, guests, and naked girls. Some of these girls wore masks to make them appear as if they were daemons, others had their faces exposed. I heard fluttering above me and saw that bats were flying free in this cavern, but none of the people there seemed bothered by this. Fires also burned by the walls. I lowered my gaze and found myself staring in disbelief at the scene in front of me. Most of the club members and guests sat in majestic armchairs, but if they needed to put their goblets down one of the naked girls would run over, bend to her hands and knees, and allow her back to be used as a table. Other of these naked girls walked around the room, flaunting their bodies to the club members and guests, occasionally bending over so that their bottoms could be flogged with a hickory stick.

My attention was distracted by club members and guests who came over to gawk at me and to ask Frankenstein questions about my construction. One of them noticed that my goblet was empty and went to refill it. When the goblet was returned I drank the whiskey quickly, hoping to dull my senses to this place. When my gaze wandered around the room, I found myself staring at a scene unfolding before me, not believing my eyes, but sickened nonetheless. One of the club members had lowered his trousers and dropped to his knees so that he could enter one of girls who was acting as a living drink table from behind. As he rocked back and forth to push himself into her, the girl showed no evidence of this happening, not in her expression and not in allowing herself to be moved even an inch.

The noxious spell holding me was broken by one of the club members elbowing me. "Pity her if she lets as much as a drop of the drink spill," he said with a wicked grin. "She knows the punishment that will be waiting for her if she does. And, my enormous friend, feel free to make use of any of these girls in the same manner. That's what they're here for! Although, I daresay, they'll have their work cut out to keep from spilling their drinks if you were to have a go at them!"

I looked away, disgusted that I had ever caught sight of it. It was then that I spotted him. He stood in the shadows, away from the rest of them. Tall, finely dressed, with his black cape and mask signifying him as a club member, and his black boots so expertly polished that they glinted. His body had an angular look to it, like a knife blade, and when I saw his dead pale eyes behind his mask, I recognized what he was. I pushed my way past the crowd that had grown around me so that I could stand next to this solitary figure.

"Do any of them know what you are?" I asked.

He turned to glance briefly at me with his dead eyes before fixing his gaze on one of the young girls being used as a drink table. Even in his fine clothing and his immaculate grooming, he held a feral quality. He did not bother answering me.

"I know what you are because I have seen your kind before," I said. "I saw them when they ran naked and wild in the forest like animals. That was where they hunted their prey, not in a club for the wealthy and bored."

He turned again to look at me. "Why are you bothering me?" he asked.

"I am simply surprised, that's all. I did not expect to see a vampyre here, or in London, for that matter, especially one dressed as you are. I am curious. Are there other vampyres like you hiding among men as if they were one of them?"

"Why, are you jealous that you will never be able to do so?"

I did not answer him, but neither did I move away from him. I could tell that my presence bothered him.

"Must you stand by me?" he asked at last, the civility in his voice strained.

"I am still curious," I said. "Can you transform into a wolf as your forest cousins did?" A bat swooped close enough nearby that I had to move my head to avoid a collision, and that caused a harsh smile to wrinkle my face. "Was that one of your brethren, or is that only a superstition?"

When he turned again to me his eyes were dark coals that held burning embers glowing hotly within them. "You have grown very irritating," he said, his voice the same hiss a snake might make.

"That may be so," I said. "But you will not be feasting tonight on that young girl whom you have been salivating over."

"And what matter is that of yours?"

"None, but she will not be your victim. At least not tonight."

He laughed at that, the sound emanating from him was something icy, something terrible. "You wish her for yourself? Is that what a creature like you feasts on, the flesh of young girls?"

"Hardly. I prefer berries and mushrooms from the forest."

He regarded me coldly, his lips pulling into a tight, bloodless smile. "Then why are you making this an issue?" he asked.

I did not attempt to answer him, for I wasn't sure myself why I was doing this.

"How would you intend to stop me? With force? My strength and speed could surprise you."

"Doubtful. I have already witnessed your kind's speed, and I am sure your strength is equally impressive. But I see no reason to do battle with you, not when I can expose you for what you are to this club. So leave now before I do that."

"And you think that would matter to them?"

"I would think so, yes."

A fury exploded in his eyes, but then just as quickly it seemed to burn out, and his eyes were back to the icy, dead, pale things I had seen earlier. He gave me a short nod.

"Very well," he said. "I will leave here, for all the good it will do. You don't think that there are hundreds of young girls out there that I can pick to feed on instead?"

"That may be, but you will not be feasting on this one."

He shook his head at me as if I were something pathetic, but did not argue any further, and I watched as he glided across the room, moving like smoke, and then disappeared through the red curtains. I wondered why I had bothered chasing him away. What I did was futile, and it amounted to little more than flailing away in a ridiculous attempt to prove that I was different from Frankenstein. The more I thought of it the more disgusted I became with myself. It was then that I spotted where the whiskey was being kept, and I moved over there so that I could pour myself enough of it to dull the thoughts that were bombarding my mind. All I wanted then was that, and to blind myself to the scenes that were playing out around me.

———

Frankenstein was in a sour mood when we later took a coach back to his flat. He was a bit drunk, and I was much more so. For several minutes he brooded silently, and then he spat out his distaste for the club. "Disgusting," he pronounced. "That those girls are there of their own free will and are paid handsomely for every welt they take on their backside and every cock that enters them! It makes the proceedings there nothing but a mockery, defeating the very purpose of what we are trying to accomplish!" His voice lowered as he stewed in his anger. "A disgrace, Friedrich, an absolute disgrace. That club was filled with nothing but imposters. Children playing their games."

"You prefer it then when innocents are taken against their will and cruelly tortured and defiled. Is that when you are happy?"

He turned angrily toward me as if he were going to strike me, but his emotions fizzled. "You don't understand yet, Friedrich. What we will be doing with our performance is striking a blow against the hypocrisy of this so-called enlightened world of ours that murders with impunity in the name of God and state, but refuses to acknowledge that we are the same as any other beast in nature." His voice trailed off into a whisper as he shook his head and added, "When you see our performance you will understand this, also." He brooded silently after that before turning to me with an inquisitive smile.

"The gentleman that you chased out of the club. Why?"

"He was a vampyre there to feed on one of the young girls. I did not care to have him do that, so I ordered him to leave."

He stared at me blandly, then shook his head. "You seemed to have found a hole in the spell, Friedrich. It appears that it is allowing you to lie to me. It is not supposed to. Fine. Keep your secret then."

With that he went back to his brooding over all of the moral deficiencies he found with the club. How they weren't sufficiently evil for his tastes.

When we arrived at the flat, and the coach driver had let us out and had driven away, Frankenstein informed me that we would be leaving early the next morning for Scotland. That he had gathered all the knowledge that he needed for the operation that he would be performing.

CHAPTER 26

When we left London, we did so by hackney coach, with Frankenstein having little care whether the driver was alarmed by my size. I was hidden within my cape, and while the driver of the coach glanced back nervously at me numerous times, he did not have the courage to say anything. When he left us at a pier where Frankenstein had chartered a boat, the driver only seemed relieved to be free of us and more than happy to drive away hastily and without making any sort of fuss.

The boat took us up the eastern coast to Edinburgh. During this trip both of us were too preoccupied to pay the other any attention; Frankenstein presumably deep in thought about the operation that he would be performing while I couldn't stop thinking of Johanna soon being brought back to me and how she would react to my new appearance. A nervousness twisted my insides as I thought of this, and my stomach seized up every time I imagined how she might scream or simply show a look of horror upon her face on seeing the hideous form that I had been made into. As much as I longed to see Johanna again, I equally dreaded the thought of her seeing me as I now was.

The boat arrived in Edinburgh late in the evening, and we spent the night at a house that Frankenstein had waiting for us. Again, we were too absorbed in our own thoughts to bother acknowledging each other, let alone speaking any words to each other.

The next morning Frankenstein had a coach take us further north to the coast. This driver also paid me quite a bit of attention, but unlike the other drivers that we had so far encountered, this one was not shy in speaking to me.

"Warm isn't in, gov'nor, to be wearing such a heavy cape as that?" he asked.

I did not bother answering him, but that didn't deter him.

"You're a big'un, aren't you? How tall are you? Seven feet? Never saw no one your size before."

Frankenstein had been absorbed in his thoughts, but this brought him to life and he snapped at this man to watch the road and not to pester me with any further questions, at least if he wanted to be paid for his services. The driver apologized, but still kept glancing back at me suspiciously. When we reached a desolate area along the shoreline, Frankenstein had the driver stop the coach. He first took a gold watch from his pocket to see the time, then got out of the coach, and after pulling a small folding telescope from out of his inside jacket pocket, used it to spy in all directions. Satisfied with what he saw, he ordered the driver to take his trunk down from the coach where it had been stored. The driver struggled doing this and several times glanced in my direction hoping that I would offer to help, which I ignored. He did not need to see that I could have lifted the trunk with one hand. After several minutes of his huffing and puffing he had it on the ground. He was then paid and told that he was no longer needed.

His expression queered as he looked about this desolate area. "You want me to leave you here in the middle of nothin'?" he asked.

"That is what I am asking."

He shrugged and climbed back on top of his coach. After he drove away, Frankenstein pointed out an island to me.

"That is where we will be going," he said. "A rowboat should be waiting for you no more than a mile down this coast. I would have you come with me, but I am afraid with your additional weight we would capsize the rowboat I have arranged for myself."

Frankenstein glanced once more at his pocketwatch as a way to dismiss me, and I turned and headed off in the direction that he was sending me. The rowboat was where he had said it would be, and I used it to row myself to the island, which was only a little more than a mile from the coast. With my great strength, the trip was quick, and at times the boat appeared to barely skim the water's surface. When I reached the island, I saw another dinghy with two men aboard also coming to the island, and I knew that Frankenstein was one of those men. From the distance they still had to travel and given the speed at which they were propelling the boat, it would take them another half hour to reach the island's shore. I left the water's edge then to quickly explore the island before returning and waiting for my enemy.

I was able to cover the grounds in less than a half hour. The island was a barren place, mostly rocks, and held little more than four small cottages. From a distance I spied a man and a woman entering one of these cottages. From the manner of their dress they must have been servants. Both appeared to be large-framed with an extraordinary dullness about them. I guess as well as being servants they were most likely also husband and wife. I did not call attention to myself so it was doubtful that they saw me.

There was a grayness about the island that not even the late afternoon sun could dispel. A shiver ran through me as I sat and waited for the other rowboat to arrive. Without looking inside any of the cottages, I knew that in one of them a girl was being held captive, the one who would be transformed into Johanna. I tried not to think of her and the terror that she must be suffering. I tried telling myself there was nothing that I could do about it; that Frankenstein's black magic held too much power over me, but I still felt myself a coward and a fraud.

It took Frankenstein and his companion much longer than a half hour to bring the rowboat to the island, as they had trouble with the waves and the undertow. The sun was already setting by the time their boat pushed onto the rocky shore. They both looked winded as they climbed out of the boat with perspiration glistening upon their faces. But Frankenstein smiled excitedly as he stepped first from the boat.

"Friedrich, I see that you beat us here," he said. "Not that that should have been any surprise. I would like you to meet a childhood friend of mine, Henry Clervil. He will be observing our experiment, and will later journey back with us to my castle."

The other man was Frankenstein's age. Tall, finely dressed, with sharp features and a sallow complexion made to appear even more so by his black hair. Like Frankenstein, he was incapable of disguising the cruelty that he held in his eyes and mouth. As I looked at him, I felt as if I had seen him before.

"Do I know you?" I asked.

His eyes showed only slightly more life than those of the vampyre's I had encountered in that depraved club in London, and the light faded quickly from them as the look he favored me with turned dismissive. "I don't believe so," he said as he left the boat to join my enemy.

Frankenstein had me carry his trunk for him, and as he walked to one of the cottages, he explained that the operation would be done the following morning. "This will be a more difficult operation than my construction of you, Friedrich. The task of replacing one brain with another while leaving the rest of the body intact is a delicate one and requires far more precision. But after a restful night's sleep, and assuming that I have a strong morning sun, I should be able to proceed."

He had me leave his trunk at the cottage where he would be residing, and then he led us to a cottage that was farthest away from the others. Inside of this one were all the instruments and devices he would need for the operation, as well as the young girl that I had chosen to be Johanna. This girl lay on a small cot, her eyes swollen and rimmed with red as if she had been crying miserably for days. She avoided looking at us. I saw that a manacle was attached to her right ankle, chaining her to the cot so that she would be unable to move more than a few feet from it, with the cot itself bolted to the floor. Frankenstein ignored her and instead opened a wooden crate. From this he removed a glass bowl, inside of which floated a lump of grayish matter in a similar milky liquid that had sustained Charlotte.

"Here is what remains of your Johanna Klemmen," Frankenstein said, his eyes intent on the contents of the bowl. "Her brain."

Clervil stood transfixed as he also stared at this bowl. I looked away. The thought of Johanna's skull having been cut open so that her brain could be removed from it disturbed me greatly. I knew she was dead at the time and would not have felt anything, but still this violation to her body struck me as utterly inhuman. And yet, the same was going to happen to this girl who lay only a few feet from me, and I was going to be complicit in the act.

Frankenstein had enough of studying Johanna's brain, and he packed the bowl away. He commented that the brain showed no signs of atrophy or decay. "It should be fine," he said. "Tomorrow, Friedrich, you will be reunited with your betrothed and we will see if her memories have remained intact. For tonight, you will stay here and keep your future bride company."

A panic seized my throat at the thought of doing this. "I would like to stay in one of the other cottages tonight," I croaked out, my voice not much more than a guttural rasp.

"I am sorry, Friedrich, but that won't be possible. I will

be occupying one of the cottages, Henry another, and the final cottage is housing my servants."

"Then I will sleep outside."

"No, I prefer that you spend the night with your future bride." A pitiless glimmer sparked in Frankenstein's eyes, and Clervil's lips also twisted into a thin smile. "I know it goes against accepted moral conventions to spend the night before your wedding with the bride, but in this case we'll make an exception. Besides, it will allow you to more appropriately reflect on the decision you have made, and your role in the events that will be transpiring. Good night, Friedrich. And I do not want you leaving this cottage. Henry and I have much to discuss, and I do not wish to be disturbed."

With that Frankenstein left. His friend, Clervil, turned once to look upon me the way a snake might a mouse, and then he also left. There was another cot along the opposite wall from where the girl lay and I sank into it, lowering my head heavily into my hands. As I sat there in my cowardice I tried not to think of the girl chained helplessly only a few yards or so from me. After some time, however, I could feel as if her eyes were boring into my skull, and that feeling soon became unbearable. I dared to glance toward her, and she was indeed staring at me. As swollen and red as her eyes were, the rest of her face was pale and bloodless.

"Am I to be your bride?" she asked in a tortured voice that pierced my heart. "Is that why you chose me and I was sent to this place? Am I to be married to a monster?"

I shook my head and lowered my eyes from hers. "No, that is not what it will be."

"Then what will it be? I have the right to know!"

"You will be made . . . different."

I could not keep myself from glancing up and seeing the confusion which wrecked her face. "How will I be made different?" she asked. Then it was as if a trace of the knowledge flickered in her eyes. "It has to do with that brain, doesn't it?"

I nodded. "My betrothed was murdered, and that is what remains of her," I said.

"I do not understand," she said. "What does that have to do with me?"

I tried to smile at her, but from the way she reacted my attempt must have made me look even more hideous. The twisting within my stomach became something awful.

"You will be made into my Johanna," I said at last.

"What are you saying?"

But she saw it. She made the connection then to her being brought to this island, all of the medical equipment and devices within the room, and my Johanna's brain being kept in a glass jar in the very same room. Her mouth gaped open, but she was too stunned to cry or weep. "All of you are monsters," she whispered in a voice that sounded like death. "You are going to take my brain and replace it with another? Is that why you chose me? To be made into something unnatural and monstrous like yourself?"

"If I did not choose you they would later commit utterly vile acts on your body and then kill you in a terrible way."

"And this is not utterly vile? To turn me into a freakish thing?"

"At least now you will live," I said.

But she knew this wasn't true, just as I did. At least she would not be living in any way that could be thought of as natural. Her mouth closed, and she aged terribly in front of my eyes. The pain within her became an awful thing to witness.

"I would rather die," she said. "My younger sister was stolen also. If they are going to murder her then I wish to be murdered also so that we may join our ancestors together. I do not wish this thing that will be done to me. It was evil of you to choose me."

She started weeping then. The sound that she made was that of a wounded animal that needed to be taken out of its misery. I sat, helpless, and listened.

"I am sorry," I said. "I wish there was something I could do to help you."

"Unlock my chains!" she pleaded as she wept. "The keys are right there on the table! Or will you have me turned into a monster for your own selfish needs?"

"That is not my reason," I implored. "Frankenstein holds a power over me that keeps me a slave to him. But I wish I could help you."

When my words made sense to her, she started wailing and beating on her head with her fists. I got off the cot so that I could keep her from hurting herself. When I came within a few feet of her, she lurched forward and grabbed me by my cape and pleaded with me to kill her. "If you cannot help me, then end my life, I beg of you!"

Once more I was being asked to kill an innocent to save them. I could not bear to turn her down. I tried to lift my hands to her throat, but Frankenstein's spell prevented me. She saw in my eyes that I was powerless to do as she begged, and she fell on the cot weeping violently.

I stepped away from her. When she had grabbed my cape I heard a crinkling noise, the type paper might make. I remembered then the odd little man I had met outside of Leipzig and the envelope he handed me. I searched the inside pocket of my cape and pulled out this envelope. It had yellowed and aged with time, and when I looked inside of it I saw dried plant leaves, and remembered this odd little man telling me that they were leaves from a jimson weed plant. I remembered what he told me about how I could use these leaves to cure myself. I looked around the room and saw that everything I needed in order to follow the instructions I was given was present. I felt an excitement as I acted once more as a chemist and generated a tincture from the leaves, and then diluted this in the method that was explained to me.

The girl had stopped her weeping to ask me what I was doing. I told her I wasn't sure. Once I had the solution prepared, I placed several drops of it under my tongue. Nothing happened, at least at first. But as hours passed and night approached I felt a sense of peace that I could not remember since long before waking up within Frankenstein's laboratory. I also realized that a noise that had been buzzing incessantly within my skull was gone. I hadn't even been aware of this noise, but the new quiet that I sensed was something welcome and unfamiliar to me.

As I sat in the dark marveling over these changes that had occurred, I remembered where I had seen Henry Clervil before.

CHAPTER 27

Early the next morning Frankenstein's servants departed the island by rowboat. I heard them as they left, and assumed that Frankenstein sent them away so that they would not be witness to what was going to be happening. It was a short time later that Frankenstein and Clervil entered the cottage. Frankenstein nodded brusquely at me and commented that he hoped I had had a good night's sleep. He was too absorbed in his planned operation to have paid any attention to what I might have said. His friend, Clervil, was the same way: both of their faces hardened with eagerness and anticipation. Neither of them paid attention to their surroundings within the cottage as they headed straight to the wooden crate where they had stored Johanna's brain the evening before. I had learned during the night that the girl's name was Mariel. If they had been paying attention, they would have noticed that Mariel's manacle had been removed, even though she remained sitting on her cot.

"I remember where I saw you before," I said, but both Frankenstein and Clervil were too caught up in their plans to bother listening to me. "Clervil," I shouted this time, "I am speaking to you!"

Clervil turned to give me a forced look of patience that bordered on exasperation, but did not say anything to me.

"I saw you in Ingolstadt," I said. "This was when I was still Friedrich Hoffmann."

"Is that so?"

"Yes, it is. In fact, it was my last night as Friedrich Hoffmann. I remember your face from the beer hall. At some point you must have stood next to me. Is that when you slipped your poison into my ale?"

He blinked but otherwise showed no reaction to my accusation. "I don't know what you are talking about," he said. He then turned away from me to help Frankenstein lift the wooden crate onto a table.

I roared then, and it was something fierce and horrible. Both of them turned around, a mix of surprise and amusement befuddling their faces. In a dizzying rush I was off the cot and moving toward them, and then I had Clervil by his jacket, lifting him so that his face was inches from mine. And now nothing but stark terror reflected in his expression. I roared again, and my face wrinkled into a horrible grin. I threw him against the wall with enough force that he went through the wooden structure and tumbled onto the ground outside. Frankenstein tried shouting something at me, but I ignored him. He would be for later. I followed Clervil through the hole in the wall that his body made, and I picked him up again. His eyes fluttered open and he opened his mouth as if he were trying to scream, but no noise came out.

"Why did you poison my ale?" I demanded.

"I-I did not! I swear—"

I slapped him across the mouth. Not hard enough to kill, or even injure him severely, but hard enough to break several teeth loose from his mouth. I knew the answer to what I was asking him, but I wanted still to hear the words from him.

"Do not lie to me or I will crush your head like a grape!"

I grabbed his skull and applied enough pressure to make his eyes bulge.

"I only did as Victor asked," he cried.

"Frankenstein sent you to poison me?"

"Yes! Yes!"

"And he sent others to defile and murder Johanna Klemmen? Or did you do this? Or did he?"

Clervil was sobbing now, and in his tears he stammered out that Frankenstein had hired others to murder Johanna.

"Stop your crying now or I will slap you again, but this time with enough force so that you will lose all your teeth!"

He stopped his crying and pathetically begged me for mercy. "Please, I beg of you, I myself have a betrothed—"

"Shut up! Why did Frankenstein want to murder Johanna Klemmen, and arrange for me to be punished for this crime? Answer me!"

Clervil squeezed his eyes shut before answering me. "He needed an educated brain for constructing you," he whimpered weakly. "When he learned of your betrothal to Johanna Klemmen, he wished also to perform this experiment to test the nature of attachment. He needed brain material from two young lovers."

He told me only what I had long suspected, but there was no longer any doubt of Frankenstein's culpability in the murders of Johanna and Friedrich Hoffmann. I threw Clervil then, sending him traveling twenty feet through the air. When he landed, he lay quietly for a moment. Then surprised that I had let go of him, he staggered to his feet, and in his panic to escape me he tripped and fell after only a few steps. His head struck sharply against a rock, and from the way his skull cracked open I knew he was dead. I left him to return back to the cottage.

The scene within the cottage showed Frankenstein cowering on the floor with his hands and arms covering his face to protect himself as Mariel struck blows at him, all the while screaming her hatred at him. I pulled her off of him.

"He deserves to die for what he has done," she forced out, her eyes simmering with her rage, her small white face shining in its violence.

"You do not need his blood on your hands," I implored her as I led her back to the cot.

She nodded. "What he has done to you is far worse," she said in a harsh whisper. "If anyone deserves vengeance against him, it is you."

I left her standing by the cot, but I did not wish her to see what was going to happen next. I found myself trembling greatly as I approached Frankenstein, my rage and hatred boiling within me. He looked at me, more confused than afraid.

"What happened to Johanna Klemmen's brain?" he asked. "The bowl is empty. How am I to bring your betrothed back to you if her brain is missing?"

For a moment Frankenstein disappeared in a haze of red, the rage blistering inside of me too great to allow me to see properly. What happened next was as if it were a dream. I was barely aware of grabbing him by his jacket as I did Clervil, or lifting him into the air so that he could witness the fury burning in my eyes. I must have carried him through the hole in the cottage for the next thing I was aware of I was standing by Clervil's body, with Frankenstein in my grasp and his feet dangling helplessly in the air. He was talking to me, trying to be patient as he kept saying over and over again for me to let him down, that the spell which he had rendered over me would prevent me from harming him. To prove otherwise I slapped him in the ear hard enough to cause it to immediately begin to swell. This stunned him and caused him to close his mouth. As I stared at him, another plan entered my mind, and I tossed him to the ground. I trembled as I told him to leave the island.

"But before you leave, I want you to look at your childhood friend, Henry Clervil. See how his brain is leaking from his skull? A pity, otherwise you could scoop it up and use it for your next wicked experiment."

He glanced quickly toward his dead friend and he whitened to the color of milk. When he looked back at me his lips trembled as if he were encased in ice.

"If I leave now you will lose your beloved forever. Do you really want that, Friedrich?"

My hands closed into fists as I stared at him and fought to keep from ripping him to pieces. I said through clenched teeth, "You are trying my patience. Leave this island immediately or I will tear each of your limbs from your body, but I will do so in a way that will keep you alive for days."

Any confusion that had remained in his face was gone, replaced instead by raw panic. He understood full well that he'd better listen to me. I watched as he struggled to stand and then as he ran to the shore, moving with the unsteady gait of a drunken man. He tripped several times in his fear, but eventually he reached the rowboats and pushed one of them into the water. It seemed to take him a great deal of effort before he was able to climb aboard it, but then he was rowing away. Slowly, but still propelling the boat away from the island's shore. Only then did I open my fist to unveil the button that I had pulled from his jacket. A great sense of weariness came over me and I turned and walked to the area where I had buried the last of Johanna's remains. I dropped to my knees and told her how sorry I was that I could not allow her to be brought back to me.

"It was not cowardice on my part, my beloved," I whispered. "I knew that you would have felt the same warm feelings toward me regardless of what body I resided in. But it would have been a wicked act to allow harm to come to an innocent girl, and I knew that you would have been repelled by me if I had allowed it to happen. I was not deaf to the words that you spoke to me in my dream. We will have to be content with spending eternity together once I leave this earth."

I mouthed a silent prayer to her, promising her that I would be joining her soon, and as I struggled to imagine my

Johanna, a hand touched my shoulder. I looked up to see Mariel standing beside me, concern wrinkling her brow.

"Is this where you buried your betrothed's remains?"

I nodded, at that moment unable to speak.

She tried to smile sympathetically at me but her exhaustion from all the evil that she had had to endure over these many months kept her from doing so. She asked about Frankenstein. "Is that fiend dead?"

I shook my head. I felt every bit as exhausted as she looked. "Clervil is," I said. "He died when he fell in his panic to flee me. I will allow others to deal with Frankenstein. Come, we need to leave this place."

She wanted to ask me more questions but stopped once she realized that I was too weary to answer her. I first carried Clervil's body onto the last remaining rowboat, then went back and searched through the cottages until I found where the food and water was kept. I then loaded the rowboat with supplies, guessing that we might be on the water for some time. I also covered Clervil's body with a sheet, and apologized to Mariel about needing to bring his body with us. She nodded, but did not say anything about it.

Once I pushed the rowboat from the shore and climbed in, I spotted Frankenstein in his boat and pointed him out to Mariel. Her face paled with hatred as she stared at him.

"He has not gone very far," she said.

"No he hasn't," I agreed. "He appears to be struggling with the waves. We might be here for a while."

"It is a good thing then that we have water and food." Her eyes narrowed as she stared in Frankenstein's direction. "And even better that he has none."

"Mariel, it might be best if you try to get some sleep. You have been through a great ordeal."

She nodded and positioned herself to try to sleep. Although she was tiny, a slender girl not even five feet tall, the boat was cramped, especially with Clervil's body on board, but eventually she was able to contort herself so that she did not touch the corpse. Although it was summer, there was little sun and a coolness came off the water, and once she closed her eyes I covered her with a blanket that I had taken from one of the cottages. And then I set about to follow Frankenstein, but also to keep my distance from him so that he would not know I was behind him.

I was right about it taking a while, for it ended up taking many more hours than I would have guessed. Either due to his panic or the fact that he was dizzy from the blow that I had struck to his ear, Frankenstein appeared to have very little strength and his boat mostly drifted in the currents. At one point he collapsed, and I worried that he might be dead. It was too soon for that. He needed to first be condemned as a murderer by his fellow man, then he could die. I chewed on my lower lip, praying that he would show some life. Mariel awoke then, and squinting toward the other boat, asked whether Frankenstein was dead.

"I do not know," I said.

We both sat watching this other boat while I let ours drift in the same current that carried Frankenstein's. After a while I took out some food and water for myself and Mariel. We ate quietly, both of us staring intensely at the apparent lifeless form within the other boat. When Frankenstein awoke from his unconsciousness and began rowing again, even though it was done listlessly, I found myself grinning. It would not be fair for him to escape his crimes that easily. I continued to follow him as his boat drifted along, with him only occasionally influencing its travel.

When night came, Frankenstein had still made little progress, and I worried that he might drift out into the ocean where I would not be able to safely follow, at least not without putting Mariel's life in jeopardy. We were many miles from the island and as far as I could tell, from Scotland, and still Frankenstein's boat continued to drift aimlessly.

"Can you still see him in this darkness?" Mariel asked. Her teeth chattered from the cool night air, and I leaned over so that I could wrap the blanket once more around her.

"I can still see him," I told her. "He appears to be having a great deal of difficulty in controlling his boat. I guess he is used to others doing his bidding for him and has little experience performing his own labors."

She looked around in the darkness, and worry showed in her eyes. "Do you know where we are?" she asked.

"I do not, but don't worry. I will be keeping the promise that I made to you last night after I unchained you. I will see you returned safely to a city before I leave you."

She nodded again, but worry lines continued to show around her mouth, which I could not blame her for. After I had found myself free of Frankenstein's spell, I searched my cape's inner pockets for jewels and gold that I had originally stolen for Henriette but kept in case I would need them at a future time, and I had given Mariel enough of these jewels to not only guarantee her safe passage back to her home, but also to make her wealthy. It would be small compensation for what she had had to suffer through.

The night wore on. As I became more afraid that I would have to quit Frankenstein or risk Mariel's safety, I spotted land and saw that my enemy's boat was caught within a current that would wash it ashore. Mariel was asleep, and I followed Frankenstein's boat without waking her. When I saw where the boat had landed, I marked the location in my mind, and then I proceeded to row as quickly as I could so that I could leave Mariel at a coastal village where she would be safe. Within minutes I traveled several miles as I sent the boat skipping along the ocean's surface and found what I was searching for. After I brought the boat to shore, I helped

Mariel off it. From the haziness of the sky it was predawn, still several hours before the sun would rise, and a small fishing village lay only a short distance away.

I was originally going to leave her there. But as I thought of how she only spoke German and did not have any knowledge of English, I had a change of heart.

"Wait here," I said. "I will be back in only a short time. I want to ensure you safe passage back to your home in Erfurt before I leave you for good."

She nodded, having been through too much already to argue with me. I left her the food and water, and then raced the rowboat back to where I had seen Frankenstein's boat wash ashore. I spotted his boat, but Frankenstein must have wandered from it for he was not in sight, nor could I see anyone else in the gray haziness of the night. I carried Clervil's body from the boat and dropped it in a clearing a few yards from where Frankenstein's boat had been left. Before leaving Clervil's body, I placed the button I tore from Frankenstein's jacket within Clervil's dead hand and folded this hand into a fist. I had earlier collected the teeth I had knocked from his mouth, and I spread these by his face, then I struck him hard enough in the jaw with an oar from Frankenstein's boat to leave an imprint, and I let the oar drop not far from Clervil's body. With that done I raced back to the rowboat I was using so I could return to Mariel, and was relieved when I found her where I had left her.

"You have done so much for me already," she told me. "You do not need to do anything more." But this was said halfheartedly, and I could tell that she was scared. Before Frankenstein's paid villains had abducted her from her home, she had never left her native Saxony.

The village was only a half mile from where we stood, and we walked there together and quickly found an inn. I put my hood up, and dropped to my knees, hoping in these early hours that I could confuse the innkeeper about my height, and then I pounded on the door until the innkeeper appeared. From the puffiness of his eyes and from the way he yawned, I had woken him from his sleep, and from the way he scowled at me he was not happy about it. Still, even on my knees I was taller and broader than most men. I placed a dozen gold coins in his palm, and his attitude quickly changed to subservience.

"I wish for my niece to spend the remaining hours of the night here, and tomorrow you will arrange for her to travel back to her home in Erfurt, a city within Saxony. The gold I have paid you is more than double what the cost should be."

"Aye, no worries, sir," he said. "I will make sure that your niece returns home safely, don't you worry."

"You had better," I told him. "I will be checking to make sure of it, and if anything happens to her the price you will pay will be very dear. She only speaks German, so arrange for her guide to be fluent in that language. And serve her a hearty breakfast in the morning!"

He nodded effusively, and I took his hand within mine so that he could see how massive my own hands were. He winced as he saw how his hand disappeared in the same manner that an infant's would within an adult's, and he promised me again that my niece would be well taken care of. I knew from his expression that there would be nothing to worry about. I then turned to Mariel and explained to her in German what I had arranged, and I repeated the promise I made to her the night before—that I would see all of the prisoners within Frankenstein's dungeon returned home safely, and that I would tell her sister, Alice, that she was safe and would be waiting for her in their home. Mariel flung her arms around me, barely reaching the circumference of my chest, and began crying and thanking me profusely for saving her. I looked away in discomfort and patted her head, and the innkeeper also showed his embarrassment even though he had no idea what she was saying.

"Don't worry, sir, believe me when I tell you I will see that she is taken good care of," he promised, and he took her by the hand and led her into his inn. Once the door closed, I rose to my feet, and after sighing heavily, I made my way back to where I had left the boat.

Before I left this place, I needed to check on the mischief that I had created, and I stole my way to the nearest village where Frankenstein's rowboat had washed ashore. This turned out to be Clogherhead, Ireland, and as I expected, Frankenstein was arrested that same morning for the murder of Henry Clervil. I spied all this from a distance, but when I saw him being accused of the murder and later taken to the jail in the city of Drogheda, I was mostly satisfied. While I would have preferred for him to answer for his true crimes, at least this would mark him as a murderer, and he would pay as dearly for Clervil as he would have for Johanna's and Friedrich Hoffmann's murders, let alone all of his other ungodly acts.

I watched as he was locked away behind bars before I finally quitted this place.

Chapter 28

For at least twenty minutes I heard the donkeys braying as they pulled the wagon up the steep path that they were being urged to travel. I tried not to think too much of this and pulled a cork from another bottle of wine. By the time the wagon had reached the top of the cliff, I had finished this bottle, and I threw it into the stone fireplace and watched as the bottle exploded into tiny glass fragments. The fireplace and floor around it was littered several inches deep with these fragments. So many wine bottles, at least a third of what had been left in a well-stocked cellar.

I sat and listened as he approached the main gate, and heard his gasps and cries when he saw the ruin that was done to his castle. He must have known I was there, but he did not flee, and instead I heard his footsteps echoing across the marble floor. To leave no doubt about my presence, I opened another bottle of wine and drank it hastily so that I could smash the bottle in the fireplace. When he heard this noise, his footsteps stopped for only a minute, and then they continued. I sat quietly after that and waited for him.

Frankenstein was as pale as a ghost when he entered the dining room. His body near emaciated, his cheeks sunken, his eye sockets gray and hollowed, his hair in disarray as if he had been caught in a windstorm. He waited silently for me to speak, his eyes near lifeless. I stared at him for a long moment before I felt that I could control myself to say what was on my mind.

"I have been waiting here for months for you," I said. "Ever since I heard of your release for Clervil's murder. I thought your conviction and death, even if done by a quick hanging, would satisfy my thirst for revenge, but now with this obscenity of your release my desire for revenge is burning hotter than ever before, and I have spent months pondering what to do."

"It was no obscenity," he said, his voice a dull, listless drone to match his wasted appearance. "I was innocent of Henry's murder."

"You were," I acknowledged. "Just as I was of Johanna Klemmen's murder, but that did not prevent me from being broken on the wheel for it, and the evidence against me was no more compelling than the evidence against you. But I was a member of the working class, and never fully understood the power of wealth, and how a wealthy father can buy a son's freedom no matter what evidence stands against him."

He remained silent, and I shrugged, not really caring what he had to say regarding the matter. "Do you like what I have done to your castle?" I asked, forcing my grin.

"Why? Was it necessary to destroy it?"

"I had months to spend waiting for you and I wanted to put the time to good use. I should commend you on your wine cellar. Very well stocked, and an excellent selection."

I tottered to my feet. He took a step backward, but did not run away. I don't think he would have been capable of fleeing; from the way he had paled his legs most likely would have given out on him.

"I am quite drunk," I said. "That is the only reason I am able to keep from killing you right now. I do not know if you have had a chance to fully appreciate the destruction I have done to this castle, but let me give you a tour."

Frankenstein stood frozen as I moved toward him. When I reached him I stood grinning harshly, and then grabbed him by the collar of his jacket, and proceeded to half carry him so that I could give him a tour of his castle. He put up no resistance to this, although I had him lifted so that his toes dragged on the floor, so I doubt any resistance would hardly have been possible. The first room I took him to had once been his evil amphitheater.

"I am especially proud of my handiwork here," I said. I twisted him around so he could view the full extent of what I had done. All the furniture within the room had been broken into pieces, and the wall that the mural had been painted on had been stripped to bare stone. The floor of the room was littered with rubble.

"You should have seen how they tried to scream when I punched holes through the mural and tore it apart," I said. "You would have thought that they were truly living instead of figures painted on a wall. If I could have left the women alone I would have, but unfortunately that was not possible, for the men all ran and hid behind the women, or at least they tried to. I have to give you credit, not only did you instill in these painted men your dark soul, but also your cowardice. As you can see, I destroyed the entire wall, and when I broke apart their figures, their faces settled into death masks. I was going to burn these pieces, but I saved them for you to see."

I picked up one of the fragments from the wall which showed the face of one of the malicious waltzing men, and he indeed looked like a corpse the way his eyes were closed and the trickle of blood that ran from his lips and the greenish tinge to his skin. Frankenstein looked at this but only blanched at its sight. I held him where he was so he could fully appreciate the extent of the damage that was done to the room, and then I dragged him to each of the closets off of the room so he that he could see that they were equally turned to rubble.

"You haven't asked about your guests," I said as I dragged him to the boudoirs on this floor so that he could see the destruction that was done to them. "They were here when I first arrived. This was when I still believed you were going to be convicted of Clervil's murder. I am afraid most of them are probably dead now, although not exactly by my hand."

Frankenstein hadn't made a sound as I dragged him from room to room to see how I had left them in ruin. I turned him toward me to make sure he hadn't passed out for I wanted him to fully appreciate the fate his guests had suffered, and when I saw that he was staring at me wide-eyed but too terrified to utter a word, I continued.

"I forced them each to select an illustration from your planned drama, and I promised them that I would act out those illustrations on their bodies if they did not within one hour's time climb down the path by foot to the base of the cliff. In their haste many of them tumbled off the cliff, and their bodies could be seen until the snow covered them. The few that made it to the bottom might have survived, but given the way they were dressed and the fact that I hadn't allowed them to take any supplies, I doubt they made it out of the Chamounix valley. Although, who knows? Perhaps one of them did. But it did seem a fitting ending for them given how anxious they were to see those illustrations acted out on others."

Frankenstein showed no reaction to this, and I was afraid that he might have slipped into a state of shock. When I slapped him to see whether he was still with me, he asked in a thin but irritable voice whether that was necessary. Grinning harshly, I dragged him up the stairs so that he could see how I had turned the living quarters into a ruin of what they had been, with every piece of furniture destroyed and every wall demolished.

"You might be relieved to know that I made sure that your honored Marquis was sent by donkey wagon back to

Paris," I said. "I wanted him alive. I did very depraved things to him, things that I am sure must have made him insane, and I wanted him to be able to live out his miserable remaining years within a lunatic asylum. I made sure to escort him personally down the path, and gave the carriage driver explicit directions where to take him, although I asked him to take the donkey wagon instead of the horse carriage."

"That is good," Frankenstein uttered in his petulant drone. "I am glad the Marquis was sent in good health."

I couldn't tell whether he was being sarcastic with me or was just too numb to understand my words, but I continued with our tour. "You might also like to know that all of your prisoners were set free," I said. "Not only that but I made sure that they were brought safely to Geneva. I used the wealth left behind by your guests so that these innocents would be compensated for what was done to them. It wasn't enough. Not nearly enough, but at least it would guarantee their safe passage back to their homes and allow them to live out their lives in comfort, and maybe someday they will be able to forget the terror that you inflicted on them."

"That was very generous of you, Friedrich."

This was said sarcastically, and I trembled for a moment as I fought to keep from breaking his neck. Thank God for the wine I drank!

"Do not say my name again," I warned him. "I won't be killing you while I give you this tour, but if you say my name again I will start breaking your bones."

He nodded his understanding of what I promised, and as I dragged him from room to room my temper eased.

"Fortunately none of the prisoners knew your name," I continued, my voice calm again. "If they had you would have been imprisoned, and I would not be able to act out my plans. At first I was willing to let society punish you for what you have done to me and Johanna and all of your other victims. But over these past months since your release from that Irish prison, my thirst for vengeance has grown and has become something nearly insatiable. No, letting a court punish you will no longer do. And now I have an entirely different fate mapped out for you."

We were done with the upper floors and I dragged him down the stone steps to the dungeon. When we arrived there he saw that his eight pillars of death had been left intact.

"Pick a number between one and eight," I told him.

He began crying then. A pitiful whimpering cry. "Please, don't," he begged. "You have already ruined me. You don't have to do any more."

I struck the stone wall with all my might, and the stone cracked under the blow. "Pick your number!" I roared.

In his fright he picked the number four.

"Ah, a coward's number," I said, as I chained him to the fourth pillar. "This one is only a quick spike through the heart. There are so many more fitting numbers that you could have picked, but no one can ever say that I am not a man of my word. Or should I say, an abomination of my word."

"I gave you life!" he cried out. "How can you act so unmercifully to the one who gave you life? And these crimes you accuse me of, they were for the greater good, both for medical knowledge, and to show the world its hypocrisy, for how can you expect man to evolve if they don't understand the nature of their cruelty!"

I had to stand very still for otherwise I would have murdered him instantly. "How dare you say these words to me," I said, my voice every bit as cruel and inhuman as anything Frankenstein had ever dreamt up. "You murdered Friedrich Hoffmann and Johanna Klemmen, and you did this not for any medical knowledge, but so that you could act as God and perform your unholy experiments. How can you dare to argue any high-minded reasons for what you were going to do to your prisoners? Evil men will always try to rationalize their acts with a higher purpose, but what you have said so far is rubbish. I saw the way you and your guests looked at these prisoners, I saw the anticipation and bloodlust burning in your faces. So do not dare tell me that you had any other reason for your planned drama than wanting to enjoy watching young girls and children defiled and murdered!"

With that I pulled the chain for this death machine. Frankenstein shrieked then, and looked flabbergasted when nothing happened.

"I disabled the gears to this evil machine," I said. "If you had nine lives, then I gladly would have chained you to each of these pillars and let you experience each death. But you only have one life. What was it Shakespeare said? *Cowards die many times before their deaths, the valiant never taste of death but once.* I will see you die a thousand times before I will allow your final death to come."

I unchained him from the death machine. His eyelids fluttered for several moments and I thought he was going to collapse, but he struggled to regain his composure and he remained standing on his feet. Without a word to me he turned and headed toward the stone steps. While his legs appeared unsteady, he did not fall, and I followed behind him. As he walked through the castle toward the main gate, he paused as if he desired to ask me a question. I knew what that question would be—Where had I hidden his collection of occult books—for I heard him earlier when he was searching through his hidden cabinet. He wisely decided against asking me this question and continued to the gate. I was tempted to volunteer the information that I had burned his prized collection and that they were now only ashes, but decided that his not knowing so would create more inner turmoil. Of course, if I had told him this I would not have mentioned the page that I had torn from the most insidious of his collection. Once Frankenstein stepped outside, he attempted to muster some dignity as he turned to me.

He cleared his throat, and with his body stiff and his expression set in a stern fashion, said, "Let this end now. No good can come of this hatred laying waste to you. Let us both imagine that we have woken up from an evil dream and try from this moment to live in peace."

I had never hated him more than I did at that moment. The two of us to live in peace? After what he had stolen from me? After cruelly murdering the woman that I had loved more than life itself? And what had he lost? Nothing more than the ability to create evil! And he dared speak these words to me as if he were leaving me as something other than an abomination to mankind!

I trembled as I stood staring at him, and once again a red haze nearly blinded me to him as my rage boiled and blistered within my soul. But it could not end this quickly. He needed to suffer many more deaths before I would finally squeeze his last breath from him. Somehow I managed to keep my hands at my sides, and while I did not answer him with words, I am sure he understood me from the raw emotion that flooded my eyes. He turned and walked away from me, and I followed him to his wagon, and continued to follow him as the donkeys pulled him down the path that wound around the cliff. I had too many plans to allow an injury to come to him now. Once the donkeys reached the bottom, I continued to follow Frankenstein and watched as he took the open single-horse drawn carriage from the stable held below. While I would have preferred him to suffer the indignity of having to return to his home by a donkey wagon, I needed him safe, and for that reason I allowed him to take the carriage. As he rode across the glacier, I stood and watched until he disappeared from sight. After that I returned to the castle, for this was going to be my home until I completed my vengeance against Frankenstein.

CHAPTER 29

Over the months that followed, I spent part of my time at the castle and the rest of it spying on Frankenstein. Occasionally I would let him see me—usually when his mood had lightened so that I could remind him of what was waiting for him. When these moments would occur he would pale, and any semblance of good humor would disappear from his face. Most of the time I would remain hidden from him, but when I absolutely needed to I would show myself to him, for I could not stomach seeing him happy for too long.

During these months Frankenstein lived at his father's home on the banks of Lake Geneva, and it would take me two days of hard traveling over the glaciers and mountains to reach this place. While I hated to give up my spying on him, at times I would have no choice. If I spent too long watching over him the hatred within me would become so fierce that I knew if I did not leave I would be unable to keep myself from murdering him, and I was not ready for that yet. When these overpowering feelings would come over me I would force myself to quit Geneva and to return back to the castle. Once there I would drink enough wine over several days to deaden these impulses. And only then would I dare to return back to my enemy.

While I had turned much of Frankenstein's castle into rubble, I did leave certain things undamaged. The wine cellar. The food pantry. The massive armchair that Frankenstein had constructed specifically for me. Most important, a hidden laboratory that I discovered deep within the bowels of the castle. This laboratory was reached from the dungeon by a secret passageway, the door to which was very cleverly concealed and that I had only serendipitously discovered.

This laboratory was as well-stocked as any apothecary's, and held the compounds that I needed. I used these to make a solution which, when applied to a handkerchief and then later pressed over a victim's nose, would cause the victim to fall into a deep slumber.

Each night that I was in Geneva, I would wait until my enemy was asleep and then I would scale the northern wall of his father's house so that I could slip into Frankenstein's room unseen. While he lay asleep I would apply my specially made compound to a handkerchief and then press it against my enemy's face. Sometimes he would wake briefly, but then his eyes would quickly drift closed, and he would fall into a deep sleep that nothing would be able to wake him from for several hours. Whether he remembered these intrusions, I could not say. I would like to think so, for that would certainly have caused a greater trepidation within his spirit the next morning. These moments were so brief that most likely if he did remember anything, he thought of them only as fragments of a troubled sleep. While he then lay unconscious, I would light a candle and take from my cape the page that I had torn from his insidious book of the occult, the one that had been wrapped with human skin, and I would chant the spell on the page over and over again. While this spell was not the same as the one he had cast over me, and would not make him my obedient slave, it would suit my purposes for when the time was right.

During the months that I observed Frankenstein he would engage in normal activities and attempt to fit in with the other people around him, all of whom appeared to be decent and kindhearted folk. This was an act on Frankenstein's part. To my eyes there was no disguising the evil that lurked inside of him. What others would confuse as a quiet and somber countenance, I knew to be defeat and cowardice. I had ruined his plans to commit further atrocities, and all that was left for him was to play this part and try to pretend that he belonged with other decent people. So he hid his true proclivities and acted as a chameleon with those around him. Most likely he was trying to fool himself as much as anyone else.

It was clear that Elizabeth Lavenza was in love with him. I could see it in the way she would look at him and how she would blush when he would hold her hand. Why she could not see him for what he was, I could not say, but he fooled all the others also. In his emaciated state and having gone through what they believed to be an appalling ordeal of having his childhood friend murdered and himself falsely accused of the crime, they looked upon him as if he were a wounded bird that needed to be brought back to health. When I would see them act this way my blood would boil, and I would be sorely tempted to quit my hiding and rush to them so that I could explain his true nature and the crimes that he had committed and the further evil that I had prevented. But I knew it would do no good, and besides, doing so would go against my plans. Still, it would rankle me to witness this, especially watching Elizabeth Lavenza act in this fashion, for she otherwise appeared to be an intelligent and generous woman.

I was not surprised when Frankenstein announced his engagement to Elizabeth, although I was actually surprised in the way he acted with her; for he doted on her and showed her only gentleness, and it mostly seemed sincere. For a long time I wondered about this, for I knew he was incapable of truly loving her, or anyone except himself. Eventually I understood his behavior. He needed to convince himself that he loved her. As long as he could grasp what she offered him, he would be able to fit in with society and pretend that he was like everyone else. What she was really offering him was a chance of normality, or at least the facade of normality.

I waited until a week before Frankenstein's impending marriage to surprise him while he strolled alone in the woods nearby his father's house. At first he nearly fell over from fright, but as I walked alongside him so that there was only a foot's distance between us, he tried to act as if I wasn't there.

"I hope you have not forgotten about me," I said.

"I have not," he answered, his voice barely a whisper.

"Good, good, for I have not forgotten you. I would congratulate you on your upcoming wedding, except it will not be a pleasant day for you. I should correct myself. The day itself might be pleasant, I cannot say, but your wedding night will certainly not be."

He tried looking at me but could not force himself to do so. I had stripped myself of my cape for this meeting, for I wanted him to remember clearly what he had turned me into. We continued walking together and Frankenstein after some time attempted to clear his throat so that he could talk.

"I am a changed man," he said at last, his voice sounding strangled. "Before, it was as if I was under a dark spell, but that spell has been broken. I beg your forgiveness and I offer my sincerest apologies for what I have done, and I promise you that I will live out the rest of my life performing acts of contrition."

I laughed at that. "In the months that I have watched you I have yet to see you perform a single act of contrition," I said. "But even if you are sincere in what you are telling me, do you think an apology is appropriate for the crimes that you have committed? My murder, Johanna's, Charlotte's, as well as all the kidnappings?"

We walked for several hundred more yards before he asked in that same strangled voice, "What would you have me do?"

"You could travel back to Ingolstadt and confess your crimes and let yourself be broken upon the wheel as I was."

The little color he had left bled out from his complexion. "They would think me a madman if I did that and they would only lock me up in an asylum," he said.

"Possibly. Still, it would be something. Or you could instead write out your confession and hang yourself by your own hand. It would be a cowardly way to end it, but at least a modicum of justice would be served."

He thought on that before shaking his head. "I could not do that. I could not hurt Elizabeth in that way."

He turned to glance at me, but I had already left his side so that I could spy on him from a distance. He stood startled with the same dazed expression upon his face that you would see on a deer that had been surprised by a hunter. He turned slowly around to search for me, and on realizing that I was gone, he continued with his walk, his gait now slower and more unnatural. As I watched him, I wondered why I had made those suggestions, for if he followed either of them they would rob me of my vengeance. I decided it was because I knew he would be incapable of showing the necessary courage to do either of what I had suggested, for he was not in any way the changed man that he proclaimed himself to be.

CHAPTER 30

From a distance I witnessed Frankenstein's wedding ceremony, and later spied on their celebration. I watched as he armed himself with a pistol and a dagger, and later as he and his bride boarded a boat on Lake Geneva. Did he really believe he could escape me by water? Had he already forgotten how I had been constructed? While the boat moved faster than any man, I had little problem in racing along the shores of the lake so that I could follow it. I was there to watch them when they departed the boat to spend their wedding night in a home in the resort town of Évian. I spied on them as they walked hand in hand along the shore, and then as they sat together. When Frankenstein's bride entered the house by herself, I stole along the outer walls so that I could go through her bedroom window and surprise her. I did this so quietly that at first she did not hear me. When she at last noticed me she opened her mouth to scream but was too frightened to do so.

"I am not here to harm you," I said, "but to convince you to abandon the fiend whom you have married."

She stared dumbly at me as if she could not understand what I was saying. I felt pity for her, but I needed her to leave Frankenstein on his wedding night. I knew it would strike a fatal blow that would send him reeling. Just as Henriette could have once been an anchor for me in keeping my thirst for vengeance in check, this woman seemed to be a similar anchor for Frankenstein; she was the only thing holding him to his false hope that he could live a normal life. If she was gone he would be set adrift. His last few months would be spent in utter turmoil.

"When Victor Frankenstein resided in Ingolstadt as a medical student, he had me and others murdered, and he later created me in this monstrous form."

She shook her head, my words finally making sense to her. "No," she insisted. "You are lying!"

"I am not lying. My name used to be Friedrich Hoffmann, my betrothed's name was Johanna Klemmen. He had both of us murdered."

I had saved several of Frankenstein's illustrations for this purpose, and I handed them to her. Her mouth gaped open as she looked at them and understood what they portrayed.

"These are Frankenstein's," I said. "He arranged for almost two hundred young women and children to be kidnapped, and these are just a few of the acts that he was going to have performed on these innocents. I have since saved them, but it is what your new husband was going to do. This is the monster that you married, and you must leave him now. I will help you."

I reached out to touch her arm, and she turned on me as a cornered animal might, throwing the papers in my face.

"You are the fiend!" she cried. "You are the monster! And you are not worthy of speaking my husband's name!"

If she had said anything other than that, I would have carried her away if necessary so that I could show her more evidence of her husband's crimes and convince her of his evil, but those words blinded me. I was lost within them and the rage that they stirred up within me. When reason came back to me she was dead by my hands. It had happened in the briefest of moments, but I had throttled her and left her sprawled dead on the canopy bed. I was still struggling to understand what I had done when Frankenstein swung the bedroom door open and raced into the room. He looked first at his bride and understood by the dark purple marks along her neck what had happened. Then he turned toward me, enraged.

"Now you know how it feels," I said.

He began fumbling for his pistol, but before he could have it pointed at me I was already out of the window and racing away. It was too early still to take my final revenge on him, and I was reeling from what I had done to his bride. Even with what she had said to me, she was an innocent and did not deserve what I did, and there was nothing that I could think of that could justify my action. All I could feel was an empty hollowness in the pit of my stomach. But I tried not to think of it, and instead only imagined how I had injured my enemy, and what would be happening next.

I allowed Frankenstein to bury his bride before I acted on the rest of my plan. The spell that I had spent months rendering upon him would draw him to me when I desired, and my plan was to bring him to the most desolate spot on the planet so that he could die alone and so that his body would never be found by man. I had been planning this for many months. More than just planning. Ever since I learned of his release from that Irish prison, this was all I had been able to think of. Now that I was finally acting on my plans, all I felt was emptiness, and whenever I would try to imagine my Johanna to comfort me, I would instead be haunted by the image of Frankenstein's bride dead by my own hands. But my following through with my plans was all I could think of, so I led Frankenstein back toward his castle. Many times I would stop and wait for him to catch up to within a mile of me before I would continue. When I reached the castle, I headed north, and used the spell to keep drawing Frankenstein after me.

This journey continued for many months as we passed through deserts and glaciers. I still had gold and jewels on my person, and at one of the remote villages I encountered, I traded some of these for fur clothing, supplies, a dog team, and a sled. Perhaps the people I traded with had never seen a European before and assumed that I was typical of other Europeans, for they showed no alarm at my sight. While the cold did not bother me, at least not in the way it did when I was Friedrich Hoffmann, I rid myself of my cape and used then only the furs that I had acquired. After leaving this village, I traveled for several hours before stopping to wait again for Frankenstein. When he appeared on the horizon I saw that he had also acquired a sled and a team of dogs.

I kept heading north, for I would take us to the North Pole itself if I had to to see my enemy drop. It was then that I passed a most peculiar thing. A ship stuck in a sea of ice. At first I wondered why anyone would attempt such a foolish trip, and then whether everyone on board had perished. This second question was answered when I saw activity on deck. I decided whatever their reason for being out in this icy wilderness was their own, and I continued on a short distance so that I could be hidden from the ship but still watch for Frankenstein. A day passed as I waited, and it was only then that I spotted Frankenstein's sled. The ice had broken where he was, and he had been set adrift. His dogs were gone and he lay seemingly unconscious on his sled. I watched as men from the ship rescued him.

I could not believe this had happened. If Frankenstein had expired on that piece of ice I could have been satisfied with my revenge, but now I did not know whether he was dead, or whether they would be restoring him back to health. For days I worried about this, and resisted the urge to steal aboard the ship to check on my enemy. If he survived I would later draw him back to me, and if he died I had to believe that I would somehow know this. So as difficult as it was, as much as the unknowing gnawed at my soul, I settled in to keep watch over this ship.

These were torturous days; the sun ever present in the sky, almost as if to mock me and not even allow me a moment of darkness so that I could attempt to sleep and escape the thoughts that were nagging at me. The journey had taken longer than I had expected, especially now with my enemy aboard this icebound ship, and I hadn't brought enough food for my team of dogs. I tried setting them free, hoping that they could find something to hunt in this wilderness, but they were too exhausted from my pushing them these many days and I had to watch as they withered and died around me, adding more blood to my hands.

I do not know how many days I kept vigil on this ship, for it was impossible to tell with the sun always in the sky, but I knew it was many, possibly several months. At one point the sea ice broke up enough to open a passage of escape for this ship, but it stubbornly remained where it was. It was perhaps two days after this had happened that I felt a shift inside of me and I knew that my enemy was dead. I had no choice now; I had to steal aboard this ship so that I could bear witness to his lifeless form. I did this carefully, and was undetected as I snuck aboard and crept below to the captain's quarters, where somehow I knew Frankenstein lay.

He was dead, as I had known he was. As I looked upon his corpse all I felt was hollow inside, for I had achieved little with my vengeance other than allowing it to consume me and twist me into something as malignant as my enemy. I remembered Brother Theodore's words when I had left his monastery; how he was afraid that my thirst for vengeance would lead to my ruin. He was right. Now that my enemy was dead I could see clearly what I had done. With my murder of an innocent woman I had doomed myself and had lost Johanna forever. I understood also why I had approached Frankenstein a week before his wedding. It wasn't to taunt him. At a subconscious level I must have been hoping that he would act on one of the suggestions I made; I must have known that otherwise I would ruin myself. He was an evil man and he deserved his death, but not by my hands and not at my ultimate cost.

It was as I was staring at Frankenstein when the door to the cabin opened and the man who must have been the captain of the ship entered. I forced myself to look away from my enemy so I could meet this man's eyes. In all of my contempt and hatred for what I had allowed myself to lose for this villain's death, I forced out in a harsh whisper, "This is my victim. In his murder my crimes are now consummated."

The look this captain gave me was one of utter revulsion. I could only imagine then the lies that Frankenstein had told this man during his months aboard his ship. With my voice strangled I said that I would leave him alone with this most worthy creature, and with that I escaped through the cabin window, landing on an ice floe that took me swiftly away from the boat.

CHAPTER 31

The ice floe carried me for many miles. I thought that I would perish aboard it, and looked forward to that fate, but eventually it brought me to a barren landscape of ice and snow. I traveled south for many days and did not die as I expected and hoped for. Instead I reached a remote village, where I was able to trade the last of my gold for supplies, animal hides, and tools. I did not bother with acquiring another sled and dog team, for where I was going I wished to be alone without even the company of animals. I loaded all of my purchases on my back and trekked until I found an isolated area by a lake, and there I set about bringing down trees and building myself a small cabin. Once this was built I decided this would be where I would wait out my final days far away from other men. The lake had fish I could catch, and there were berries and nuts and mushrooms in the woods nearby to further sustain me.

I had not slept for months, at least not more than a few minutes at a time when I would drift into unconsciousness while I kept my vigil over that ship, and even before then, I had slept little while burning for my vengeance over Frankenstein. That first night after I finished constructing my cabin I slept fully and deeply, and had no dreams.

As the days passed, whether I slept or not I would spend the nights laying on my bed of animal hides, and as dawn approached I would leave my cabin and perform my daily chores, which amounted to gathering firewood and nourishment, although some days I would take on projects, such as constructing crude furnishings for my cabin. Once my chores

were completed I would sit by the lake and pray for forgiveness for the murder I had committed and for my betrayal
of Johanna.

Years passed as I lived this way and waited for death,
but death's release seemed to escape me. I did not age, nor did
I get sick. During this time I was not once able to dream of
Johanna. While my dreams were generally serene, I prayed
that she would visit me once more, but this never happened.
When I would remember that one dream I had had of her
when I was held within Frankenstein's castle, I would remember how she told me that she was afraid that she would
lose me, and tears would come to my eyes. Not over my own
loss, but of how I had abandoned her.

I do not know how many years had passed when my
peace was invaded by a foreign and unpleasant noise that
made me think of how rampaging elephants might sound. I
sought out the source of this noise, moving swiftly from my
cabin and through the woods nearby. The scene that I came
across sickened me. Dozens of women and children stood
huddled with a few old men among them. They were close to
what I knew were vehicles, except they were too large and
had no horses to pull them. I would later learn they were
motorized transport machines and were the source of the
noise that had disturbed me. What sickened me was the sight
of the soldiers. Their uniforms had a special malignancy
about them, and they were setting up what I knew were
weapons, although they were of a sort that I would never
have imagined. They were there to slaughter defenseless victims. Women and children and old men! When I heard them
speaking my native German I was outraged! Was this what
my fellow countrymen had degenerated into, to commit such
horrific atrocities?

I broke a heavy branch from a tree and threw it with all my might at them, knocking down two of them, perhaps even killing them. The third of them turned his weapon toward me and it spat out metal that ripped my flesh and bit cruelly into me. This injured me greatly, but in my rage I still had enough strength to rip down another branch and throw it at him, and saw that the blow crushed his skull.

The ones who were going to be massacred were now safe. I had little strength remaining in me. I turned and struggled to make it back to my cabin so that I could die in peace. I wondered if that was what had kept me alive for all these years, to save these people as a way to help atone for my crimes. I collapsed on the ground a mile from my cabin and crawled the rest of the way, but I did not die. Over time my injuries healed. Death still would not come to me.

Through the years, my solitude was to be more frequently invaded by what I knew were man-made objects passing through the sky that made a similar unpleasant rumbling noise to those motorized vehicles. I would later learn that these were airplanes, but for a long time I could not fathom what their nature was.

I do not how many years had passed when my longing to visit Johanna's grave became something I could no longer ignore, no matter how unworthy I felt to do so, and I set out to travel back to Leipzig. For many miles I was able to travel through undisturbed woods. From the little I had already witnessed, I knew the world had changed, but I could not possibly be prepared for what I saw when I entered the new world of man. It was staggering, as I looked upon the size and construction of new buildings and how vehicles flew by at unimaginable speeds and how man now lighted his cities to make nighttime little

different than day. It was difficult navigating through
these cities unobserved and I tried to avoid other people,
but it was not always possible. Still, I reached Leipzig, and
while much of the city had changed, the church where
Johanna was buried still stood and her grave remained
undisturbed, although her grave marker was so badly worn
that it was difficult to make out her name upon it, even
with the full moon brightening the night sky. But while I
could not read her name I could still feel the engraved letters. Even without that, I would have known that this was
where she was.

I had brought an armful of wildflowers and I placed these
on her grave, then fell to my knees weeping. I begged her forgiveness. "I am so sorry, my beloved," I cried. "God had
tested me greatly, but I failed and I ruined my path to you.
Perhaps someday I will be able to cleanse my soul enough
where the path will once more be opened to me."

It was hours before I had the strength to leave Johanna's
grave. As I stole though the city a sight stopped me in my
tracks. Staring at me through a bookstore window was my
enemy's name. Frankenstein! I had to retrieve this book, and
I broke into this store to do so, and also took several books
that would explain to me how greatly the world had changed
since my exile.

After leaving the store, I found a lighted place where I
could read in solitude, and my hands trembled as I read
the lies that Frankenstein recounted to Captain Walton
during his last remaining months aboard the icebound
ship. I understood the reason for this; my enemy knew he
was dying and he sought to protect his reputation, regardless of how soiled it truly was. But he also sought with
these lies to injure me. He must have had that motive given
the crimes that he attributed to me, the only one of which
I was guilty being the murder of his innocent bride. Cap-

tain Walton for the most part accurately recounted my words to him, but he misunderstood my reason for them, and he greatly embellished what I had said. Maybe in his fear he believed we had had this more dramatic conversation as was recounted in the book. Perhaps Frankenstein's lies were so deeply embedded within his mind that he could not imagine the conversation being anything other than what he wrote.

As I read this book to completion I marveled at Frankenstein's cunning and deception, even during his last moments. If I were to believe Walton's words, which I have no reason not to, then Frankenstein even went as far as to forge letters from an imaginary Felix and Safie to support his outrageous story! And he must have done this before I had sent him chasing after me!

I threw the book in the gutter after finishing it, and as I began my travel back to my remote home, I realized I needed to tell the true story of Frankenstein to counter his lies. I turned back to the center of Leipzig to steal steal paper and writing instruments, and then began my long journey back to my cabin.

During my travel I forced myself to remember all of it. Most of it I had long forgotten or tried to forget, but as I concentrated to recall these events they crystallized in my mind as if they had only just happened, and I was amazed and sickened. I had gone through what no man could have ever imagined, and while at times I had saved the lives of innocents, I had also committed grave evil. I did not blame myself for the helpful push that had sent the devil worshippers and Frankenstein's guests to their deaths, but there was no justification for my murder of Elizabeth, nor of how I had allowed my obsession with vengeance to twist me into the same abomination as Frankenstein.

When I returned to my cabin, I took pen to paper with

every intention of exposing the truth, even if it exposed my-self in the process. I believe my crimes are severe enough to keep me forever from Johanna, but perhaps one day I will be judged differently. At least I can pray that God will take pity on me and my failings.

PROPERTY OF
KENAI COMMUNITY LIBRARY